THE FLOODS 13

THE ROYAL FAMILY

Colin Thompson

illustrations by the author

RANDOM HOUSE AUSTRALIA

This work is fictitious. Any resemblance to anyone living or dead is just lucky. If you recognise yourself in this book, you should probably keep very quiet about it unless you want to make people jealous. If that is something you want to do, then tell everyone and you will instantly convert your friends into enemies.

A Random House book
Published by Random House Australia Pty Ltd
Level 3, 100 Pacific Highway, North Sydney NSW 2060

www.randomhouse.com.au

First published by Random House Australia in 2014

Copyright © Colin Thompson 2014

The moral right of the author has been asserted.

Addresses for companies within the Random House Group can be found at
www.randomhouse.com.au/offices

National Library of Australia
Cataloguing-in-Publication Entry

Author: Thompson, Colin, (Colin Edward)
Title: The royal family
ISBN: 978 1 74275 532 8 (pbk)
Series: Thompson, Colin (Colin Edward). Floods; 13
Target Audience: For primary school age
Subjects: Witches – Juvenile fiction
              Wizards – Juvenile fiction
              Magic – Juvenile fiction
Dewey Number: A823.3

Design, illustrations and typesetting by Colin Thompson
Additional typesetting by Anna Warren, Warren Ventures Pty Ltd
Printed in Australia by Griffin Press, an accredited ISO AS/NZS 14001:2004
Environmental Management System printer

Random House Australia uses papers that are natural, renewable and recyclable products and made from wood grown in sustainable forests. The logging and manufacturing processes are expected to conform to the environmental regulations of the country of origin.

The Floods Family Tree

KING   QUEEN

As it says in THE FLOODS 12, if you don't know who all the FLOODS are by now, you should be ashamed of yourself.

It also excuses you for maybe not having read all the earlier books, but that was then and this is now and it's no more Mr Nice Author.

Dedication

The Floods 13 is dedicated to the memory of Corey Lake
(2000 – 2013)

Corey will forever be the Official Number One Floods Fan and the bravest person I have ever met. You will always be alive in our memories.

Prologue

Nigel Davenport, 42¾, had an epiphany. Not an everyday sort of epiphany like when you realise you actually like brussels sprouts, but a Big Epiphany. On Thursday, while getting dressed, he realised that he was actually Nigella not Nigel, which, coincidentally, his mother blamed on eating too many pickled brussels sprouts.

He wasn't sure if this had anything to do with his deafness or the weather being much damper than was normal for that time of year. Nor was he one hundred percent sure if he had always been a lady. After all, his mother, Ironica, had, like him, also started shaving at the age of twelve. He decided that before he went any further, he should probably find out exactly what a lady was.

All Nigella and her mother knew for certain was that they were now both very confused, though neither of them were half as confused as Nigella's wife and Ironica's husband.

In an attempt to sort things out, Nigella enrolled in a tango course and Ironica started making a huge model of the Umpire State Building out of recycled banana skins.

Meanwhile, back in Clackmorton-de-la-Zouch, Lady Crustine Plantepott has been looking at herself in the family mirror.

Obviously, things could not go on like this.

Something had to be done.

Nigella decided to take drastic action and take up Highland Dancing when, by a stroke of luck, he realised it was all just a trick of the light and he was actually Nigel after all, which later tests proved to be the case. He then had to spend the next three months swapping all his buttons and button holes back again and undergoing bagpipe adoration de-programming therapy.

'As I always say,' he said, 'every cloud has a bacon lining, except the rubbish ones that are lined with silver. Or is it saliva?'

Now read on . . .

Nerlin, King of Transylvania Waters and the world's top wizard, paced back and forth in the topmost floor of Castle Twilight's highest tower. From here, he could see his entire kingdom, which he had ruled over since returning from exile several years before to overthrow the evil dictator, his beloved wife Mordonna's dreadful father, King Quatorze.

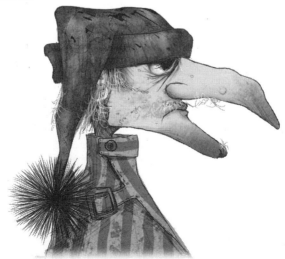

Nerlin went on to reclaim the throne for the true kings of Transylvania Waters, descendants of the great line of wizards that included the legendary Merlin himself, who now lived with his wife – Mrs Merlin – in a delightful cottage on the edge of the famous Lake Tarnish, a mere five minutes away from the capital city of Dreary, where Castle Twilight stood towering over the narrow streets like a huge green cauliflower balanced on a bundle of decaying celery.

The mountains that ringed Transylvania Waters enclosed it like a pair of loving hands, keeping it securely hidden from the outside world. The furthermost mountains were no more than a misty grey blur dotted with thin lines of smoke drifting up from remote communities that were spread throughout the kingdom, but, even in their blurriness, they gave Nerlin and everyone else living in this magical kingdom a wonderful feeling of security with added contentment. The ring of mountains was more than a physical barrier from humankind – it was bursting with all sorts of demons, old crones, pointy sticks and unpredictable spells.

Each Transylvania Waters community was unique, with every village having a speciality that no one else had.

There were, for example, the inside-out weavers of Llandango, who made magic baskets for keeping things out rather than in. These weavers were not to be confused with the outside-in weavers of Ffandango, who wove normal useful baskets but kept their stomachs on the outsides of their bodies for easy cleaning access.[1] Quite why the Llandangolites kept on producing these year after year was one of Transylvania Waters's many mysteries, as there was no record of anyone ever buying their inside-out baskets. In fact, anyone who was unfortunate enough

---

[1] *See the back of this book for a list of some fascinating communities that lived in the high valleys surrounding Transylvania Waters. And by the way, if you're expecting to see a picture of an outside-in weaver, you'll be disappointed. If you really want to know what their stomachs looked like, go to your nearest dog-food factory and check out the dustbins for the bits they reject before they are made into human burgers – that is, burgers for humans to eat, not burgers made of humans.*

to visit Llandango actually paid money not to own one. The baskets were piled up in their thousands all around the village, gradually sinking into the ground and taking root where their willow branches had originally grown. If anyone ever got a headache – which, of course, the Llandangolites never did on account of them being wizards – there were enough willow trees to make every single inhabitant of the country fourteen thousand and seventeen aspirins each.

The Llandangolites may never have sold a single basket, but they lived happy, comfortable lives, as did everyone in Transylvania Waters. This was simply because all Transylvania Waterians were wizards and witches and had more than enough magical powers to make sure they were never hungry or cold, or in need of bacon or the very latest in mobile phones, pitchforks and socks.

It was a beautiful autumn afternoon, as was every afternoon in this enchanted kingdom.[2] The

---

[2] *Except for the beautiful spring evenings, beautiful summer evenings and beautiful winter evenings.*

sun was hovering above the mountain tops making everything glow like gold, and because Transylvania Waters was a land of magic, real gold oozed out of the ground everywhere the sun shone. And the gold was reflected in the autumn leaves that were getting ready to drop dead, leaving the trees cold and naked but happy, for the approaching winter.

The air was filled with the comforting smell of bonfires, and in a tree just below the window two skylarks were singing one more song before packing up and flying down to Africa for Christmas. Far away a distant church bell sounded, which was only there to add to the romantic atmosphere, as there were no religious organisations or churches of any sort in the whole country. In actual fact, the sound came from a rather upmarket ice-cream van calling the faithful to partake in exotically flavoured sorbets and gelati.[3]

---

[3] *This is the plural for 'gelato', which is yuppie speak for ice-cream. This is not to be confused with Gelatoe, which is a disease of the foot. My favourite Transylvania Waters gelato flavour is Bacon and Chocolate Surprise, which isn't like that pretentious yuppie chocolate that is nearly black, but is lovely rich milky stuff bursting at the seams with happiness and cholesterol.*

7

'It doesn't get any better than this, does it?' said Queen Mordonna, coming up from behind Nerlin and putting her arms around his shoulders.

'Mmm,' Nerlin mumbled. 'I suppose not.'

'You don't sound like you agree,' said Mordonna. 'What's the matter?'

'I'm tired,' said Nerlin. 'I've had enough of being King. I want to retire. I want to go high up into the mountains to the Enchanted Valley of the Impossible Waterfall,[4] and build a little cottage by the river, just for the two of us, and we'll keep chickens and ducks and quail and do gardening and watch the birds.'

Mordonna was quite surprised at this. It wasn't as if being the King of Transylvania Waters had ever been particularly hard work, apart from the bit at the beginning when they had kicked out her awful father and his even awfuller girlfriend, Countess Slab, and sent them to Rockall, and even that hadn't been especially tiring, though they had been without bacon for four days.

Since then, there had been no wars or riots or trouble of any sort. After all, any problem in Transylvania Waters could be fixed pretty quickly with some magic. In fact, ever since the Floods had returned to Transylvania Waters, the country

---

[4] *See* The Floods 12: Bewitched.

had been overrun with happiness, contentment and bacon, and an enormous percentage of the population spent huge amounts of time keeping ducks and chickens,[5] doing gardening and watching birds,[6] and Nerlin had been one of the most enthusiastic.

The birds, who had been used to getting shot and eaten for centuries, had become very confused when people had stopped trying to kill them and started watching them.

'It's creepy,' said one of the magpies, 'the way everyone keeps staring at us.'

'They're up to something,' said a sparrow.

'At least when they were hunting us, you knew where you stood,' said the magpie.

'Until you got shot, that is,' said the sparrow.

---

[5] *Some people even kept quail.*

[6] *Transylvania Waters's top-selling book was* Gardening for Birdwatchers. *Transylvania Waters's second bestselling book was* Birdwatching for Gardeners. *Nerlin himself was working on a book called* Chicken- and Duck-Watching for Garden Birds, *which his publisher predicted would outsell all others, including his classic* Duck-Watching for Chickens.

'Yes, but then you'd find that out when you fell down dead,' the magpie replied.

'So, have you spoken to your eldest son about becoming King?' Mordonna asked.

'Valla?' said Nerlin. 'Not directly. I said I'd like to retire and he said he could understand that. Being King isn't a job he'd ever want to do.'

'Oh.'

'Though he did tell me he'd think about it, if he was able to introduce a blood tax,' Nerlin added.

'A what?'

'Everyone in Transylvania Waters would have to give him a small glass of their blood once a month,' said Nerlin. 'But no one would ever agree to that.'

'Apart from the Haemorrhaging Nuns of the Bloodlet Street Monastery,' said Mordonna.

'Yes, but there are only seventeen of them

and they're weird,' said Nerlin. 'I suppose Valla just said that because he knows he'd never get away with it.'

'There's only fifteen nuns left now,' said Mordonna. 'Someone said that two of them got a bit over-enthusiastic during the last full moon and drained themselves completely.'

'Anyway, I think we can assume that Valla does not want to be the next ruler of our great land,' said Nerlin.

'But surely wanting to be King is irrelevant, isn't it?' said Mordonna. 'It's a matter of duty.'

'For humans, it is,' said Nerlin. 'Can you imagine the havoc a wizard could create if they were forced into the job? Remember when your fifth cousin, Prince Wireworm, was made to take over the throne of Puritania after his father got toasted by a dragon?'

'Oh yes, I'd forgotten,' said Mordonna.

'Hardly surprising when you think about what happened,' said Nerlin. 'It's too horrible to keep in your memory any longer than you have to.'

When Prince Wireworm's father had ruled over Puritania, it had been an idyllic kingdom equal to Transylvania Waters in happiness and with even better weather. Winter only lasted for one afternoon – the third Friday in February – and it only rained for thirty minutes every day around 2am, when everyone was asleep. Everyone fell in love with the person of their dreams – even One-Eyed-Lumpskew, the ugliest person in the country, who had very weird dreams – and they all lived happily ever after until that fateful day of the dragon toasting, which had been a combination of unfortunate events and accidents after Prince Wireworm's father had made a poor choice of fancy-dress. No one had told the dragon that the King was dressed as a marshmallow and, like every sensible creature with easy access to fire, the dragon had been happy beyond measure when he had come round the corner at the annual castle fete and seen the biggest marshmallow imaginable. Before anyone could do anything, the King was a toasted gooey dead thing and Prince Wireworm took over the throne.

However, the Prince did not want to be King. He wanted to admire cabbages and play computer games, particularly computer games that involved cabbages. He did not want to make important decisions and be wise and clever. All he knew were cabbages and the occasional brussels sprout. Broccoli was beyond his realm of knowledge and even cauliflower was completely foreign to him. The happiest day of his life had been when, at the age of forty-seven, he had been awarded the Grand Order of the Golden Savoy Cabbage, a medal that he had worn outside his underpants for the rest of his life.

Unfortunately there was one other thing that Prince Wireworm was good at, and that was having tantrums. Not feeble little human ones that involved throwing himself on the floor and screaming, but spectacular wizard tantrums that involved melting the floor and dissolving entire mountains, and making lakes boil and boils burst in torrents of green slime that could drown entire villages. When he had been proclaimed King, Prince Wireworm had the greatest tantrum ever, and by the time he had finished tantrumming the once beautiful paradise that had been Puritania was transformed into a derelict rubbish dump in a really rundown part of a depressed industrial town just outside Belgium, and all the Puritanians, including the Prince himself, had been turned to dust.

So it was hardly surprising that Nerlin and Mordonna agreed that whoever was chosen to rule Transylvania Waters had to be really keen to do the job, or at least have very reduced tantrumming tendencies.

'I wouldn't worry too much about it,' said Mordonna. 'We've got five other children who could do the job. One of them is bound to want to.'

'Six,' said Nerlin.

'What?'

'Six,' Nerlin repeated. 'We've got six other children, apart from Valla.'

'Yes, I know that,' said Mordonna, 'but there's no way we could let Betty take charge.'

'Why not?' said Nerlin, who had a soft spot for his youngest child.

15

'She's a right little madam. It would be total chaos,' said Mordonna.

'Oh, I think you're misjudging her,' said Nerlin.

'No, darling, it's you who is misjudging her,' said Mordonna. 'All those pretty blonde curls and big blue eyes don't fool me for a minute. She's turned out to be quite evil.'

'Isn't that what witches are supposed to be like?'

'Not towards their own mothers,' Mordonna snapped. 'No, there's no way our youngest child is ever going to be Queen of Transylvania Waters.'

'OK, so moving on,' said Mordonna. 'Who's next after Valla?'

'Well, I'm not sure,' said Nerlin. 'With humans, the succession goes down through the boys, so I suppose it would be Winchflat.'

'Yes, but you know it's not the same with wizards,' said Mordonna. 'We are far more liberated than that. It goes down by age, then boys or girls. We haven't had any of that sexist rubbish since the Dark Ages.'[7]

So it meant that the next in line to the throne was Satanella.

---

[7] *This was true and obvious, really. As every wizard knew, humans were stuck in the Dark Ages.*

'I can see a problem there,' said Mordonna. 'You know and I know that Satanella is our daughter and we love her dearly, but she looks like a dog, barks like a dog and sniffs trees like a dog, and loves nothing more than chasing red rubber balls. Of course, inside that little dog is an enchanting girl, the victim of an unfortunate accident with a damaged wand and a bad prawn.'

'Yes.'

'And we also know,' Mordonna continued, 'that it would take mere moments to turn her back into a human-looking witch. I blame myself, really. I should have changed her back when she was a tiny baby, before she was old enough to know any different.'

'True,' Nerlin agreed.

'But we both know she likes being a dog and doesn't want to change now.'

Nerlin nodded. He would never have considered doing anything to upset his eldest daughter, though the thought of having puppies for grandchildren filled his heart with sadness.

Mind you, they would be great fun to play with, he thought, *and we wouldn't have all that awful nappy-thing to go through first, either.*

'So I think we'll have to skip Satanella,' said Mordonna. 'I must say, she'd do an excellent job, but lots of people would have a hard time accepting a small black hairy dog as the head of state.'

'Especially human beings,' said Nerlin. 'Can you imagine her at a Heads of State conference?'

'Yes, but what is really funny,' said Mordonna, 'is that some of the human leaders would be better off with a collar and lead on.'

What neither Nerlin nor Mordonna had taken into account was that time can change things. Because Satanella had decided to be a dog, they assumed that was how she would always feel. Everyone had long since stopped talking about it. So no one had the faintest idea that a little voice inside Satanella's head was wondering more and more what it would be like to be a person.

When I was a puppy, she said to herself, *I thought like a puppy. Chewing slippers and chasing rubber balls were the most important things in the whole world. Peeing on the carpet and leaving little poos behind the sofa were the highlights of my day.*

But things change with time, and it had been months since Satanella had pooed indoors. She even had her own spell to open the back door whenever she wanted to go out, and instead of going right in the middle of the lawn she now went and hid in the bushes.

'Though if they think I'm going to bury it with my own feet,' she said to no one in particular, 'they can forget it.'

The stopping-being-a-dog feeling continued to grow, but Satanella kept it to herself. And then one day, as she came back from her daily walk around the town, she realised that she had not stopped to sniff a tree or a lamppost even once. The strong smells had still called out to her as she passed them, but they had lost their magnetic attraction. Not one of them, not even the tree outside Goldie's house, had excited her.[8]

---

[8] *Goldie was a handsome but dumb labrador with a stupid, pathetic, typically unimaginative name that only a labrador owner would come up with. Satanella was almost tempted to do a spell to turn Goldie's fur black.*

'Right,' she said. 'That's it. Time for a change.'

Ignoring the small birds that teased her every morning as she walked across the main courtyard, Satanella went up the main steps and back into the castle. She found her parents in the library, where they were performing spells to turn all the rubbish books into really good books, using Nerlin's speciality of making sure that every single book contained at least twenty-seven references to bacon.

'Mother, Father,' Satanella said, 'I have made a decision. I want you to change me into a person.'

Nerlin was delighted. So was Mordonna, though she was slightly cautious.

'Now you're absolutely sure about this, darling?' Mordonna said.

'Well, if she doesn't like it, you can always change her back into a dog,' said Nerlin, showing once again that he knew nothing about the finer points of magic.

'No, sweetheart,' said Mordonna. 'One of the fundamental laws of magic is that whilst you can change into different species, you can only be any

22

particular species once. So, Satanella, in your case, if you don't like being a person, you won't be able to change back into a dog.'[9]

'Oh,' said Satanella. 'Well, that's all right. I've made up my mind. I don't want to be a dog anymore.'

'She could always change into a cat if she doesn't like being a person,' said Nerlin.

'Yes,' said Mordonna.

'Or a hamster,' Nerlin added.

'Quite.'

'Or a weevil.'

'Mmm, yes.'

'Or, umm . . .'

'Yes, yes, we get the point,' said Mordonna.

---

[9] *Nearly all people, including most wizards, do not know this, but there is something that is FAR MORE POWERFUL than regular wizard magic. It is called ULTIMATE SUPER-WIZARD POWERS, and those who have heard of it do not believe it actually exists, BUT it does, as we shall soon discover. See the back of this book for a chart comparing Pathetic Human non-powers, Standard Wizard powers and Ultimate Super-Wizard powers.*

'I know that,' said Satanella. 'But I've decided I want to be a person.'

'You're absolutely sure?' Mordonna asked.

'Yes, definitely.'

Satanella asked if she could choose certain things before she changed, like her hair colour or the size of her bottom or if she could have a spare arm.

'No,' said Mordonna. 'They're controlled by your genes.'

'But I wouldn't want my hair to be like what it is now,' said Satanella. 'All wiry and shedding everywhere and full of fleas and earth. Actually, I wouldn't mind the fleas. They're quite tasty.'

'Don't worry, darling,' Mordonna reassured her. 'That's dog hair. You will have person hair, probably like mine, though not as lovely, of course.'

And that made Mordonna think. Supposing Satanella turned out to be more beautiful than her? Whilst she definitely didn't want a daughter who was ugly or lumpy or both – after all, what would the neighbours say? – she didn't want Satanella to be more desirable and gorgeous than she was.

Maybe I could do a little spell to make her nose have a bump in it or give her a slight limp? Mordonna thought.

'Oh, and by the way, Mother,' Satanella said, 'don't go doing sneaky little spells to make my nose have a bump in it or give me a bit of a limp or anything like that.'

'As if I would, darling, my own daughter,' Mordonna said.

Nerlin suggested that they gather the family together to tell them what was going to happen. So it was agreed that they would all meet just before midnight by the lily pond in the secret garden at the back of the castle.

This is not a door, and if it was, you wouldn't want to go through it because there's nothing in there.

'Not the secret garden everyone knows about,' said Nerlin, 'but the secret, secret one that only the family can get into.'

As midnight approached, Mordonna did the Get-Rid-Of-All-The-Clouds-And-Make-It-A-Full-Moon Spell and the secret, secret garden was bathed in a beautiful eerie blue light.

'Ooh, look at that lovely beam of beautiful eerie blue light,' Simple Townsfolk said as he and his wife walked home from the pub. 'I bet our beloved royal family are in their secret, secret garden a-doin' of some clever magic.'

'Ooh arr, I bet you're right,' said Mrs Simple Townsfolk. 'Maybe they're changing that dog they keep sayin' is their daughter into a real person.'

'Don't be ridickerlus,' Simple Townsfolk replied. 'You been a-drinkin' too much of that nettle cider.'

What Simple Townsfolk didn't realise was that Mrs Simple Townsfolk had second sight, which is like ordinary sight without using your eyes.

'Is everyone here?' said Mordonna, when everyone was there.

'Yes,' said everyone.

Mordonna explained what was going to happen.

'First of all,' she said, 'we'd better take your collar off.'

'Couldn't I keep it? I've had it forever and I thought it would make a great belt,' said Satanella.

'Well, it might, darling, but if you measure your neck I think you'll find your waist is going to be a bit bigger than that.'

'Don't you dare do a Fat Spell on me, Mother,' said Satanella.

Mordonna was quite tempted, but reluctantly decided against giving her daughter any defects. After all, Satanella was a witch and there was no way of knowing how powerful her magic or temper could be after she'd changed from being a dog.

Once her collar was off, Mordonna told her daughter to get inside a big paper bag.

'No way,' said Satanella. 'I want to see exactly what you're doing.'

'Are you sure?' said Mordonna.

'Absolutely. Come on, get on with it,' said Satanella.

'So you're quite happy for everyone to see you wearing exactly the same as what you're wearing now?'

'Mother, I am not wearing anything,' Satanella snapped before figuring it out. 'Oh umm, yes, well,' she said, and climbed into the paper bag.

Mordonna picked up her best wand – not the one that could make Vegemite taste nice, which of course was a pretty powerful device, but the really powerful one that could change bank managers into real human beings.

She had one last read of the spell, shut the book, closed her eyes and began to chant an ancient witches' chant that came from before the dawn of time and sent shivers down the spine of anyone or anything that heard it, even worms that haven't got spines.

'Aren't you going to say abracadabra?' Satanella called from inside the paper bag.

'No, darling, no one says that in real life,' said Mordonna. 'It's just something humans say in pantomimes.'

'Oh, say it, please,' said Satanella.

'But I don't need to,' Mordonna explained. 'It doesn't do anything. It's just a silly made-up human word.'

'Oh, go on.'

'OK, OK, if you insist. Abracadabra, abracadabra.'

Nothing happened.

'And the other bit,' said Satanella.

'Other bit?' Mordonna said.

'Kalamazam, kalamazoo,' Satanella said. 'Go on. You have to say all of it.'

Mordonna looked up at the moon, sighed, took a deep breath and shouted:

'ABRACADABRA, ABRACADABRA,
KALAMAZAM, KALAMAZOO!'

Three sparrows that had been sleeping on a nearby branch turned into Christmas puddings and landed on the ground with a soft thud. In the castle kitchen, three Christmas puddings that had been sitting on a shelf in the puddings larder turned into three rather nice digital cameras.

And somewhere in Belgium a taxi turned into a side street.

Mordonna returned to her wailing.

Inside the paper bag Satanella wriggled, and then she began to giggle the sort of giggle someone who is very ticklish would do.

30

'Ahh, ooooohhhh, ahh, oh, oh, oh,' she said followed by lots more giggles, cries of 'stop it', more giggles and a lot of wriggling.

A wet patch appeared in the bottom of the bag, and suddenly a human-looking foot covered in beautiful smooth skin with no sign of a single curly black dog's hair anywhere poked through the soggy paper.

'Are you all right, little sister?' said Valla.

'Phew,' said Satanella, and the paper bag collapsed in a heap and stopped moving.

'The trouble was,' said an incredibly beautiful head as it popped out of the crumpled bag, 'that the bits of me that were still a hairy dog kept tickling the bits of me that weren't.'

'And are there any hairy dog bits left now?'

said Mordonna, hoping there were so that her eldest daughter would be a bit of a freak. If the rest of Satanella was as gorgeous as her foot and her head, then Mordonna would most definitely not be the most beautiful witch in creation anymore.

'No, Mother. You will be delighted to hear that I am totally covered in gorgeous from head to toe,' said Satanella, knowing full well that her mother would be the opposite of delighted.

'But then,' Satanella added, 'how could I be otherwise, with such a stunning beauty as my mother?'

This, of course, made Mordonna happy and angry at the same time, which was exactly what Satanella knew would happen. Betty handed her sister some clothes, and a couple of minutes later Satanella climbed out of the remains of the bag.

She was, as Mordonna had dreaded, staggeringly beautiful, not just beautiful to witches and wizards, but beautiful like a human movie-star dressed up as a witch.

'WOW!' everyone said, thought, cursed and/or muttered.

Betty took Satanella inside the castle and up to her bedroom, where there was a full-length mirror. On their way they passed thirteen castle servants, all of whom fell immediately in love with her.

'WOW!' said Satanella. 'How hot am I?'

'Extremely,' said Betty. 'Mother is going to be so furious.'

'I know,' Satanella giggled. 'Bonus!'

Now, you might think that Betty would be jealous of her far more beautiful sister, but she wasn't. Betty had always been very pretty herself in a totally non-witch way and was delighted to have a lovely big sister to do sister things with.

Satanella had been fine as a dog, but after ten minutes of throwing sticks and red rubber balls, there wasn't much else they could do together. Betty did have her human friend Ffiona, but even Ffiona's own mother – a very old-fashioned person who thought cardigans were exciting – had to admit her daughter was a bit nerdy. Ffiona would never go down to the shops and try out all the lipsticks and perfumes like other girls.

And anyway, Betty had her one true love, Prince Bert, who had eyes for no one else.[10] But there were problems with Prince Bert:

1. Apart from several strange creatures covered in sticky fur and gravy, Prince Bert was the first person Betty had ever been in love with and, as everyone knows, your First True Love is NEVER going to last more than a month/week/day/hour/minute or second.[11]

2. Like lots of young people in love for the first time, Betty had told EVERYONE about Prince Bert and now she was having second/third/fourth and fifth doubts, which she was feeling a bit embarrassed to admit.

3. Betty knew that she could do MUCH BETTER than Bert.

---

[10] *See* The Floods 12: Bewitched.

[11] *Think of your First True Love and cross out the ones that don't apply. If you have not yet had a First True Love, you can find one at your local shopping mall buying zit cream at the chemist.*

34

4. Bert knew he would never end up with anyone remotely as brilliant as Betty.[12]

5. Lots more stuff.

'You know what I'd like to do?' said Satanella. 'I'd like to go down to the shops and try out all the lipsticks and perfumes and all the clothes, especially the ones our mother is too old to wear.'

'Great idea,' said Betty. 'But first, there's something we need to sort out.'

'What?'

And, with perfect timing, there was a scratch at the door.

'OMG!' said Satanella. 'Tristram.'[13]

'Yeah, Tristram Jolyon De-Vere Creak,' said Betty. 'Your boyfriend.'

'Well, no, er, umm, not really,' said Satanella, thinking that now she was a staggeringly beautiful witch, she would probably have her choice of every

---

[12] *This was proved to be true when Bert ended up marrying Princess Kolesteroll of Siberia, who used to carry him around tucked between her third and fourth chins.*

[13] *See footnote 10.*

unattached wizard in the universe. 'I mean, we only just met recently, you know. It's never a good idea to rush into things.'

'I only met Prince Bert a few days ago too, but I know he is THE one and we will be together for, like, ever and ever,' said Betty, trying very hard to ignore the little voice inside her head that was saying *yeah, right!* in the sort of voice that really meant *NOT!*

'Well, yes,' said Satanella, 'but it's different for me. I mean, for a start, I'm older than you and when I met Tristram we were both dogs, and all dogs care about is what each other smells like. They don't care about the important things in life, like being tall and handsome and cool.'

'I've no doubt Mother could change Tristram into a wizard,' said Betty. 'And I expect he'd be just as gorgeous as you, so you'd still be perfect for each other.'

'Yeah, well,' said Satanella, 'I think I'll just wait for a bit. And don't you dare say anything to Mother.'

But outside the door, little Tristram Jolyon De-Vere Creak had heard every word and was

heartbroken. When he realised that dogs couldn't cry like humans and wizards, he was even more heartbroken. His tail, which had been wagging with sheer happiness since he had first met Satanella, drooped between his legs like a wet dishcloth.[14] He let out a tiny whimper and slunk away.

I shall leave and no one will ever see me again, he said to himself. *Not that they'd care. I would go and join the Foreign Legion if I knew what that was. And then, when everyone realises I've gone – if they ever do – they'll discover why, and they'll all hate Satanella and she will be so full of guilt she will pine away and die of a broken heart.*

'But what about Tristram?' said Betty back in the room. 'He'll be heartbroken.'

'Oh, come on,' said Satanella. 'He's a dog. The first lamppost he sniffs, he'll forget all about me.'

My sister may look like a very beautiful witch, thought Betty, *but she is still as shallow and uncaring as a saluki.*

---

[14] *At least it covered his bottom, which made everyone else happy.*

3

No one noticed the small miserable dog as he slipped through the shadows and out of Castle Twilight into the damp little alleys of Dreary.

This is where I belong, Tristram thought, *in the neglected alleys with the dustbins.*

A scraggy black cat hissed at him, but he was too sad to respond.

'Hey, mongrel, I hissed at you,' the cat said.[15] 'Aren't you going to chase me up a tree?'

'Whatever,' said Tristram.

'Whatever?' said the cat and hissed again.

Tristram tripped over a stick and fell face-first

---

[15] *In Transylvania Waters all animals can talk, even cats, which are actually quite popular with witches and wizards on account of them being selfish animals who love no one but themselves.*

into a puddle. He lay there thinking it was no more than he deserved. The cat sat down beside him and stared at him.

'Something tells me,' the cat said, 'that you are not the happiest puppy in the basket. It's not because I hissed at you, is it? I didn't do it to upset you. It's just what cats do to dogs. It's tradition. It's expected of us.'

'No, it's not that,' said Tristram.

'So, what is it then?' the cat asked. 'Lost your red rubber ball?'

'No.'

'Well?'

'No one loves me,' said Tristram.

Something told the cat that Tristram Jolyon De-Vere Creak was not your average dog. Your average dog usually has at least one person who loves them and, quite often, lots of people who do. That's what dogs are for, to make people happy.[16]

---

[16] *That, and to fetch dead birds when humans hunt them down, and to join up with other dogs to pull sleds along, and to bark at strangers, and to steal dirty nappies, and to keep old ladies' laps warm, and . . .*

'What is your name, dog?'

'Tristram Jolyon De-Vere Creak,' said Tristram Jolyon De-Vere Creak.

'No, seriously,' the cat said, laughing.

Tristram got out of the puddle and told the cat his story.

'Wow,' said the cat. 'So you're a real prince. Delighted to meet you. I am Flapwig.'

'And you laughed at *my* name?' said Tristram. 'Yes, I'm a prince. Fat lot of good that's done me, hasn't it?'

'And the girl you loved, the princess Satanella Flood, who I have had the honour and pleasure of being chased up many trees by, has now changed into a person?' Flapwig asked.

'Yes.'

'But she won't get her mother to change you?'

'No,' said Tristram.

'Well, I reckon even if you got another witch to change you – which you probably could – you'd be mad to still want her after the way she treated you,' said Flapwig.

'I know,' Tristram whimpered. 'But I love her.'

'Now that's something I'm sure I can help with,' said Flapwig. 'Follow me.'

She led Tristram across town through a network of dark half-hidden alleyways, where no one could see them.

Finally, they came to the edge of Dreary, where the houses ended and the landscape changed to scrub and wasteland. Crumbling away amongst the greenery was a group of derelict buildings that had been abandoned after the evil King Quatorze had

been deposed. It had been the secret place where the King and his cronies had hidden their enemies away and tortured them with feathers dipped in Vegemight.[17]

The roofs had fallen in, the windows and doors had been smashed to pieces and plants were gradually swallowing what was left. Now the ruins were home to a colony of stray cats.[18]

A large ginger tom emerged from a doorway and approached them.

'Hey, Flapwig, you know the rules,' he said.

---

[17] *Which is like Vegemite, only far less positive.*

[18] *Now, as everyone knows, cats are evil creatures. If you think cats are lovely, you have been totally taken in by them pretending to like you. The truth is that they're only 'nice' to you to get stuff like food and warmth. If it were the middle of winter and VERY cold, your cat would sleep in the warmest place in your house – your face. Then you would suffocate and die and your lifeless body would go cold. Then your cat would go sleep somewhere else. THAT is how much your cat loves you. Despite how popular cats are with witches and wizards, there are some that even witches can't love and other cats that simply want nothing at all to do with people. These are the ones that Tristram was being taken to visit.*

'We're not allowed to bring any outsiders here unless they're edible.'

'Yes, yes, I know all that,' said Flapwig. 'But this isn't your average stupid dog. This is a wizard – a royal prince, even.'

'Yeah, right,' said the ginger tom. 'And I'm the Lord High Chancellor of Bogwater.'

'I'm quite prepared to believe that you come from a place called Bogwater,' said Flapwig. 'It suits you. Nevertheless, this small dog before you is a real royal prince and a real wizard.'

'Prove it,' said the ginger tom, who had a very, very short tail and was called Gorsehinge.

Tristram lifted his head towards the cat and, with little more than a twitch of his left eyelid, gave a nod. The ginger tom rose up off the ground.

'Yeah, well,' said Gorsehinge, 'anyone can do that.'

But as the ginger tom continued to rise, he began to look worried.

'OK, OK,' he finally said as he passed three metres, 'maybe everyone can't do that, but . . .'

43

At five metres, he began to look pretty scared.

At ten metres, he agreed that Tristram could be a wizard, but said he knew at least five magicians who could do the same trick who were not wizards.

At twenty metres, he stopped moving and speaking.

'So, am I a wizard or not?' said Tristram.

'Maybe,' said Gorsehinge.

'Oh, for goodness sake,' Flapwig snapped. 'Of course he's a wizard, you idiot.'

'He obviously needs a bit more proof,' said Tristram, who by now was feeling considerably cheered up.

The feelings of desolate sadness that had been dragging him down were being replaced by an altogether far more exciting sensation.

Revenge.

For a split second, the cute little doggie expressions that filled Tristram's everyday face were replaced by a flash of evil with eyes of fire. It lasted for such a

brief moment that no one saw it.

No one except Gorsehinge, that is.

It caught him, as it had meant to, right between the eyes and filled him with terror. The ginger tom, who had been the undisputed leader of the stray cats for as long as anyone could remember, wet himself. And just to make his point, Tristram flipped him upside down so that Gorsehinge wet his own face.

Then he dropped him.

In a puddle.

Full of dead worms.

For a few seconds there was complete silence. The other cats had always been scared of Gorsehinge, but the sight of the old bully on his back, in the mud, stinking of his own wee, was just too much and they all burst out laughing.

Gorsehinge crept off into the bushes. In one brief moment he had lost all his power. The first thought that came into his head was also revenge, but then he remembered how his tail had become very, very short the last time he had tried to get even with a wizard. He still had nightmares about it.[19] So while Gorsehinge might have been very angry, he was not very stupid. He decided his best course of action was to swallow his pride and to try to make up with Tristram Jolyon De-Vere Creak.

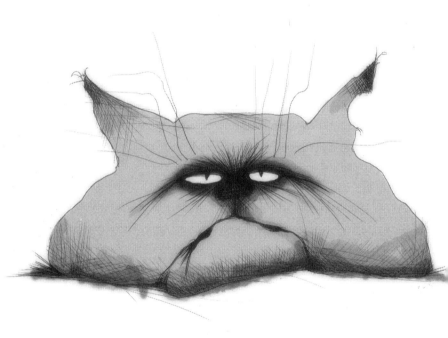

---

[19] *These terrible dreams took place in the middle of a very dark night and involved two enormous black horses, some rope and a bacon slicer.*

'Sorry,' Gorsehinge said, using the word for the first time in his life.

The effect was amazing. All the other cats gathered round him and began to lick his fur clean, even the bits with wee on.

'I'm sorry, too,' said Tristram. 'I realise I don't look like a prince or a wizard.'

The two animals sniffed various interesting bits of each other and surprised each other by becoming good friends.[20]

'So what do you want do?' Flapwig asked.

'When I left Castle Twilight,' Tristram replied, 'I wanted the ground to open up and swallow me, then you came along and brought me here. I was as low as I could go. No one cared about me. And now here I am, in this lovely overgrown place with all of you, my new friends.'

'Well, you see, that's one huge advantage being a dog has over being a person,' said Gorsehinge.

---

[20] *Yes, I know, it's amazing – a cat and a dog becoming good friends. But don't forget this was happening in Transylvania Waters, the land of magic.*

'If you were a human, wizard or not, you would still be crying into a cup of cold tea and curling up into a ball wanting to die.'

'A ball?' said Tristram. 'What sort of ball? A red rubber one?'

'No, no,' Gorsehinge continued. 'It's just a figure of speech. My point is that because you're a dog, you are genetically programmed to be happy. It only takes a few minutes to cheer up. See?'

'I do, I do,' said Tristram. 'Now tell me more about the ball.'

He may be a prince and a wizard, thought all the cats, *but he's still a dog – dumb as cardboard.*

'I mean,' Gorsehinge added, 'are you sure you want to change? Are you sure you wouldn't be happier staying as a dog?'

'Absolutely,' said Flapwig. 'Look how miserable and complicated life can be if you're a human. Name one thing they've got that we haven't.'

'Thumbs,' said Tristram.

'Yeah, well, OK. There is that,' the cats all agreed. 'Thumbs would be good.'

'iPads,' Tristram added.

'Eye pads?' said Flapwig. 'Why on earth would you want pads on your eyes?'

'Just imagine,' said Gorsehinge dreamily, 'what we could do to mice and birds if we had thumbs as well as claws.'

The cats imagined how wonderful life would be with more blood and gore and not having to swallow all those feathers.[21]

And Tristram imagined how fantastic life would be if he could throw his own ball.

'Well, you're a wizard, aren't you?' said Flapwig. 'Could you do a spell to give us thumbs?'

'OMG!' said Gorsehinge. 'That would be brilliant. We'd still be cats and dogs, but we'd have a fantastic secret weapon. There'd be nothing to stop us. We could take over the world.'

---

[21] *There are actually cats with thumbs. They are a genetic mutation known as polydactyl cats. There are polydactyl dogs too, but they can't do things such as hold doorknobs, like some polydactyl cats can. Though I once had a poodle that could play the accordion.*

'My mother made me promise that I would never do any big magic stuff without asking her first,' said Tristram.

'And where is your mother now?' Gorsehinge asked. 'Can anyone hear her looking for her missing son?'

No one could.

'Has anyone seen Tristram?' said Queen Anaglypta.[22]

'Who?'[23]

'My son,' said Queen Anaglypta. 'The one who looks like a little dog.'

'You've got a son who looks like a little dog?' said all the people who had said 'who'. 'That's

---

[22] *For those of you who have not read* The Floods 12: Bewitched *(yes, you know who you are – and so do we), Queen Anaglypta is Tristram's mother and she is the Queen of Shangrila Lakes. Want to know more? Well, read the book. AND pay the statutory fine of twenty-seven pieces of bacon.*

[23] *This was what practically everyone said when Queen Anaglypta asked them.*

amazing. Our beloved Queen Mordonna has got a daughter who is a little dog.'

'*Was* a little dog,' said a servant who had been there when Satanella had been transformed into a person. 'She is now a staggeringly beautiful princess-witch.'

'Maybe your son got changed at the same time,' someone suggested. 'That often happens with magic. I think it's called the Enchanted Echo Effect.'

'You just made that up,' said someone's wife. 'Ignore him. He does it all the time.'

But he hadn't. There really is an Enchanted Echo Effect.

'Is he a small terrier dog with blond fur?' a different someone asked.

'Yes, yes. Have you seen him, then?' asked Queen Anaglypta.

'No.'

'So how do you know what he looks like?'

'Just kidding,' said the different someone who had recently won Teaser of the Year at the International Festival of Japes and Wheezes, which

is one of the most exciting events in Belgium's annual calendar of interesting things.

'I saw him creeping out of the castle a few hours ago,' the teaser continued to report. 'And so sad and miserable he looked, dragging his tail through the puddles. It filled my heart with sadness.'

'Puddles?' said Queen Anaglypta. 'I didn't know it had been raining.'

'They were his own puddles, Your Majesty,' said the teaser. 'He'd stop, do a puddle and then walk back and drag his tail through it. Even the sparrows were laughing at him.'

The Queen and quite a few other people too were beside themselves with grief. Anaglypta was overwhelmed with guilt, underwhelmed with sadness and whelmed in quite a few other places with a bad conscience. She had been so in awe of meeting her famous relatives the Floods for the first time and coming to Transylvania Waters that she had almost forgotten her own son, Tristram, the sweet caring boy – OK, OK, the sweet caring *dog* – a devoted child who had never given her a moment's trouble.[24]

She'd seen how Satanella Flood and her son had instantly taken to each other, and the Queen had dreamily wondered if they might even get married and unite the Floods and the Creaks with litters of adorable puppies. It had crossed her mind briefly to wonder if the two dogs, who were not really dogs but a wizard and a witch, would actually have puppies or some sort of weird homunculus. But Queen Anaglypta's brain was not a place where problems and worries ever spent much time, so she had – as she always did with anything that was in the slightest bit difficult – simply forgotten about it ASAP.

Now her little boy was missing, and when someone told her how Satanella had rejected him, Queen Anaglypta realised that he was not just missing but broken-hearted too.

---

[24] *Actually, when he had been a puppy, Tristram had a bad habit of chewing chair legs with the result that sometimes people ended up on the floor with a look of sudden surprise on their faces and hot soup in their laps, but then everyone usually fell about laughing, so maybe it wasn't a bad habit after all.*

'I blame myself,' she said. 'I should have changed him into a person when he was born.'

But no one would let her have a nice wallow in self-pity.

'It's not your fault,' they said. 'It's because of that selfish, spoiled Floods girl.'

And when the news of Tristram's disappearance reached Castle Twilight, even Mordonna had to agree.

'We will send out a search party,' she said, 'and when we find him, I will turn him into an unbelievably handsome prince who any girl would swoon over.'

Anywhere else this would have been a good plan, but things were different in Transylvania Waters. The main difference was that every living animal, right down to nasty slimy slugs, could understand speech. They could use it too. This had happened many centuries before, when the original Merlin had thought the world would be a much happier and more peaceful place if every living creature could speak to each other.

It had been a bad move.

Within a few years several animals had become extinct, and hundreds of species that had been happily eating each other were now either feeling really guilty or really hungry. Here is an example:

Big ugly dangerous animal with ferocious teeth and claws is about to kill and eat very small cute animal with no defences whatsoever.

'Hello, lunch,' says the big dangerous animal.

'Hello,' the small cuddly animal replies. 'Would you like some lunch?'

'I would indeed,' says the big dangerous animal.

'Well, I've got some daisies, some lovely moss and a very early variety of beetroot,' says the small cuddly animal.

'You've also got a delicious-looking neck,' says the big dangerous animal, and bites its head off.

The small cuddly animal does not say anything on account of its talking bits being chewed up and swallowed.

'Owwwwwwwww . . .' the big dangerous animal hears its lunch screaming inside its tummy.

So, instead of enjoying its lunch, the big dangerous animal feels horribly guilty, but not enough to turn vegetarian, though it does get nasty indigestion and that particular species of small cuddly animal soon becomes extinct.

This and other sorts of problems made Merlin try to undo his magic, but it was too late. All he could do was stop everyone from understanding each other by making them speak different languages or speak in whistles (birds), grunts (pigs) and tweets (birds that don't whistle and humans who need to get a life), depending on their species.

Everyone, that is, except for the creatures of Transylvania Waters, which all knew the old wizard only too well and weren't falling for any of Merlin's magickery a second time. They alone had retained the power of speech.

So when Mordonna had announced her plans for a search party so that she could turn Tristram into an unbelievably handsome prince that any girl would swoon over, a magpie that had been sitting outside on the window sill had overheard and understood every word. This same magpie had previously been sitting on top of the castle gatehouse when Tristram had slipped away into the dark alleys of Dreary. It had watched his encounter with Flapwig and followed the two of them out of town. Then it had got bored, which happens all the time to magpies,

and had returned to the castle because it had the best bacon rind in the entire country.

'And I like to think,' the magpie would say to anyone who would listen, 'that I am a bit of an expert when it comes to bacon.'

The magpie then had two choices: he could either fly off to tell Mordonna and Anaglypta that he knew where Tristram was and would be willing to lead them straight to him for a huge reward, or he could fly back to Tristram and tell him that both queens were looking for him.

Hmm, thought the magpie, *tough choice.*

Obviously the huge reward thing seemed like the best idea, but then the magpie realised there was nothing he actually wanted.

I mean, he said to himself, *there are only three things I've ever wanted in life – bacon, girlfriends and shiny things – and I've more than enough of all of them.*

Which was true. Outside the castle kitchens was a huge oak tree. It was the magpie's kingdom, and jammed into every crack in the bark were bits of bacon rind. For five generations the magpie and his forefathers had been storing their surplus bacon here. Some of the rind was so old, the tree had begun to absorb it. On warm summer evenings, the lane on the other side of the castle garden wall was filled with couples saying to each other, 'Can you smell bacon?'[25]

This enormous treasure house of bacon meant that the magpie had so many girlfriends, he couldn't remember all their names.

And as for shiny things, well, it would take a whole book to list each and every one of them, including the places in which they were hidden. All magpies are addicted to shiny things and this one was no different. The Castle Twilight magpie, being the king of bacon and bigger than all the others, had more shiny things than anyone else. In fact, he had collected so many that there was no room for him in his own nest and one dark night he fell out. The whole nest collapsed, showering him in twigs,

---

[25] *And whose heart would not skip a beat at those words?*

bottle caps, broken glass, precious emeralds, priceless handmade watches and Christmas beetles. So he didn't need any more bling.

'I am totally blinged out,' he declared.

Of course, he could just tell the two queens where Tristram was and not bother with a reward, but he had his position in magpie society and he couldn't risk being laughed at for being kind. To a magpie, kindness was like pecking a baby bird's eyes out so that it couldn't see the inside of your throat while you were eating it.

So what could he make out of telling Tristram that there were people looking for him?

Chaos and confusion, that's what, the magpie thought.

And if there is one thing a magpie likes more than bacon, girlfriends and bling, it's chaos and confusion.

Apart from more bacon.

So the magpie flew back to the wasteland at the edge of town, where Tristram was telling the stray cats about his life in Shangrila Lakes.

'**O**i, dog,' the magpie called down from the safety of a thin branch high up in a tree.

'Magpie, lunch, kill!' the cats shouted together.

'Shut up, you stupid scraggy ratbags!' the magpie shouted. 'Or I'll tell all the posh cats in town you've made friends with a dog.'

A gigantic silence fell across the clearing, followed by a medium-sized silence that had been hiding behind a bush.

'That's better,' said the magpie. 'I've got some information for the dog.'

'Yeah, go on then,' said Flapwig.

'Tell me this,' said the magpie. 'Of all the creatures in our beloved Transylvania Waters, who do you hate the most?'

'Well, humans, of course,' said Flapwig.

'And witches and wizards,' Gorsehinge added. 'They're like humans, only worse.'

Everyone agreed. Tristram wasn't so sure. After all he was a wizard himself

'But I like humans,' he said. 'They give me dinner and throw sticks and things.'

'Yes, but just think how much better it could all be without them,' said Flapwig. 'You could have loads more dinner and any stick you've ever wanted.'

'Only if I had thumbs,' said Tristram.

'How come?'

'Well, I couldn't open the tins without thumbs,' said Tristram.

'But you could catch things and kill them and eat them instead,' said Flapwig. 'It would be

much better for you. Besides, those tins are full of chemicals.'

'Why does the dog want sticks?' asked one of the cats.

'I don't know,' said Flapwig. 'It's a dog thing. It's always confused me. If the humans like the sticks so much, why do they keep throwing them away?'

'And why on earth do dogs keep bringing the sticks back to them?' asked Gorsehinge.

'It's a game,' said Tristram.

'Throwing a bit of dead tree around is a game?' said pretty well every cat there.

'Yes, it's great,' said Tristram.

'You're an idiot,' said Gorsehinge.

'HELLO,' shouted the magpie. 'Can we get back to the point?'

'Which is?' Gorsehinge asked.

'Basically, it's this,' the magpie replied. 'Dog, what is the one thing you want at this very moment more than anything?'

'Revenge,' said Tristram.

'Brilliant,' said Gorsehinge, deciding he actually quite liked Tristram. 'Spoken like a true cat.'

'Well, I can help you,' said the magpie.

He told them how Mordonna was organising a search party to find Tristram and that she was planning to turn him into a handsome prince. Being a magpie, the bird was full of cleverness and craftiness, so he left out the bits about Tristram's mother, Queen Anaglypta, being distressed at her son's disappearance because he knew it would make the little dog run straight back to the castle.

'So, how many of you are there?' said the magpie.

'Twenty,' said Flapwig.

'No, twenty-seven,' said a voice from the back.

66

'Wonky George has just had seven kittens.'

'Wonky George?' said Tristram, who didn't know all that stuff about mummies and daddies and babies. 'Why's he called that?'

'Because George is a girl,' Flapwig explained.

'So why isn't he called Georgina?' said the magpie.

'Because that's his dad's name,' Flapwig said. 'Don't ask.'

'OK,' said the magpie. 'Let's start again. How many grown-up cats are there who can go out and distract people?'

'Probably about fifteen,' said Gorsehinge. 'Sixteen, if we include Daft Victor.'

The magpie then told the cats to spread out around the castle and to intercept the members of Mordonna's search party. Each cat would tell a different group of searchers that they knew exactly where Tristram was and offer to lead them to him.

'There will be a prize for the cat who leads people the furthest away from Dreary,' said the magpie.

'Prize? What sort of prize?' said one of the cats.

'Something small, furry and delicious,' said the magpie.

'Still alive?'

'Mostly.'

'So, while all that's going on, where will I really be?' Tristram asked. 'I want to do something. I mean, it is supposed to be my revenge, after all.'

'I have a cunning and devious plan for you,' said the magpie.

'Brilliant, great, fantastic, wonderful,' said Tristram. 'What?'

'We will go to a witch, one that the Floods do not know of, and get her to change you into a really handsome prince,' said the magpie. 'Then you will return here, where we'll get Satanella to fall in love with you and then you will throw her aside like an old dishcloth.'

'Brilliant, great, fantastic, wonderful,' said Tristram.

'Do you know a witch the Floods won't have heard of?' said Flapwig.

'Not as such,' said the magpie. 'That's the only little flaw in my brilliant plan.'

'Not so little, really,' said Gorsehinge. 'I mean, it's the entire plan, isn't it?'

'Well, yes, but I haven't started looking yet,' said the magpie. 'I've only just thought of the brilliant plan.'

'You know,' said Tristram, 'you don't actually have to find a witch the Floods haven't heard of. You could just find one who hates them.'

'Yes,' said the magpie, 'but who?'

'There are a few,' said Gorsehinge with a knowing nod, 'though most of them have been disposed of by our beloved rulers.'

'What, you mean, killed?' said Tristram.

'Yes.'

'By the Floods?'

'Yes.'

Tristram was overwhelmed. 'But I thought they were lovely, kind people and everybody adored them,' he said.

'Of course you did,' said Flapwig. 'They've

spent a lot of time creating that image.'

'Don't forget,' said Gorsehinge, 'that they are witches and wizards and the rulers of this incredible country. Do you really think they've got to where they are today by being sweet and kind to everyone?'

'But the King –' Tristram began.

'Oh yes, King Nerlin,' said Flapwig. 'He's as soft as luxury toilet paper, but he's just a figurehead. It's his wife, Mordonna, who is the real power in this country, and I can assure you that there are a lot of witches and wizards and assorted creatures who would be only too happy to see the back of her.'

'I can't believe it,' said Tristram. 'I mean, I've seen the back of her, and it's nothing special.'

'What?' said several cats at once.

'Her back's quite nice, but the front of her is much more interesting,' Tristram explained.

So if anyone had doubted that Tristram was a true prince, their suspicions were now put to rest. Only a genuine royal prince would be thick enough to think that Flapwig had actually been talking about Mordonna's back when he had said there were people who would be happy to see the back of her.

The poor little dog was completely confused. Why would looking at Mordonna's back make anyone happy? He didn't like to ask, so he just kept quiet, which showed he wasn't quite as stupid as the average prince.

'We will have to be ultra-super cautious about this,' said Flapwig. 'We can't just go round asking people if they don't like the Queen. The Floods are very crafty and clever. They have spies everywhere.'

'Wow!' said Tristram.

'We could go round asking everyone if they'd like to make a donation to buy the Queen a big present because she is so lovely,' Gorsehinge suggested. 'And if someone says no, we can ask them why not, and then depending on what they say, it might give us a clue as to who doesn't like her.'

'Or who hasn't got any money,' said the magpie.

This was a good plan. Everyone said so. Except for the simple fact that it was a useless plan.

'Yeah,' said Flapwig, 'we might even get some money too.'

'The only problem is,' said Wonky George, 'who the hell is going to give us any money? I mean, we're not nice little children collecting for a charity. We're cats – not pampered fluffy kitty cats but the type nobody wants and the ones that get stones thrown at them.'

'In that case, we'll just have to go with Plan B,' said Flapwig.

'Brilliant!' said Tristram.

'And what is Plan B?' said someone, anyone and everyone who wasn't called Tristram.[26]

Once again they were back at square one, but as they sat under a bush, looking out across the rubbish-covered wasteland, a big pile of rags walked out of the trees.

'What's that?' said Tristram. 'Is it dangerous? It smells like a barrel of pig's pee.'

'It's just Gertrude,' said Flapwig.

'Who?'

'Gertrude Flood,' said Gorsehinge.

---

[26] *Or Flapwig.*

72

'Flood?' said Tristram. 'Do you mean she's one of the Floods?'

'Yes, some crazy old seventh cousin.'

They explained that when the Floods, who had been imprisoned in the drains below Dreary, had finally escaped and overthrown King Quatorze, who had trapped them there, Gertrude had stayed

behind. Everyone else couldn't climb out of the stinking drains quickly enough, but Gertrude had lived there all her life and couldn't imagine anywhere else she would rather be. Quite a few of the Floods had been born in the drains too and had only seen the light of day through the gratings above them, but Gertrude was not like the others. In fact, she was not like anyone else at all.

When everyone had been trapped there, Gertrude had refused all offers to make her life nicer, like clean undies – or, really, any undies – food with no mouldy bits and something soft to sleep on that didn't leave you covered in slime. Then, once everyone had left, she had retreated to the furthest drain to live alone with her very weird dreams, an assortment of mysterious creatures and her grandmother's skeleton.

'I wonder what she's doing up here,' said Flapwig.

'Yes,' said Gorsehinge. 'It must be ten years since she was last here, and that was when we had that earthquake.'

74

'Maybe there's another earthquake coming,' Flapwig suggested.

'Hey, old lady,' the magpie called out from a branch above her. 'What are you doing up here?'

'Where? What? Who said that?' said Gertrude.

Because she was over one hundred and ninety years old, Gertrude was too bent over and frail to look up to see the bird. The magpie flew down and landed in front of her, but her eyes were so worn out that all she could see was a black blurry shape.

'Hello, little rat,' she said.

The magpie swore. Being called a rat was a terrible insult. It was dangerous too, as some of the cats began running around looking for the rodent.

'I am not a rat,' said the magpie. 'I am a bird.'

'What's that, then?' said Gertrude. 'Is it a kind of rat?'

'Listen, old lady, do I look like a rat? Am I covered in fur? No. I'm covered in feathers. Black lustrous feathers of amazingly shiny beauty, I might add,' said the magpie.

'What's them, then?' Gertrude asked.

75

'What?'

'Feathers. What's them, then?'

When the magpie told her, he then had to explain what a bird was. The old lady said she didn't believe him.

'Rats can't fly,' she said. 'Only one thing can fly and they be bats.'

'And flies,' she added. 'They can fly too.'

In the end, the magpie said that he was a kind of bat and that seemed to satisfy Gertrude.

'So, what are you doing up here?' asked the magpie. 'The cats said that you've been here before when there was an earthquake.'

'Earthquake?' said Gertrude. 'The earth quakes? Is it frightened of something?'

The cats joined in the conversation, but that didn't help. Gertrude Flood seemed so ancient and decrepit, and had lived alone for so long, that no one could get any sense out of her. This, of course, was merely a disguise to cover up the fact that she was actually as sharp as a very smooth pebble disguised as a piece of pointed flint.

'Look, it doesn't matter why she's up here,' they all finally agreed. 'The important thing is, can she do magic?'

Gertrude said she could and, to demonstrate, she turned a nearby tree into a bacon sandwich with tomato relish. She assured them that she could easily turn Tristram into a human, but the little dog wasn't too happy with the idea.

'I don't mean the being-turned-into-a-handsome-prince bit,' he explained. 'I mean having it done by her.'

'I see your point,' said the magpie. 'But I don't think we've got any other option.'

'What's the worst that could happen?' said Gorsehinge.

'I could end up as anything,' said Tristram.

'But we could get her to change you again until you were a handsome prince,' said Flapwig.

'Not if she turned me into an ugly prince,' said Tristram. 'You can only be a particular species once, and I wouldn't think a handsome prince is a different species to an ugly prince.'

'Probably depends on just how ugly you were,' said Gorsehinge.

They thought about it, talked about it, and then thought and talked about it some more until they ended up in exactly the same place they had been half an hour before, except everyone was now thirty minutes older.

'Suppose she changes me into a girl?' said Tristram.

Everyone said that was impossible, though no one was prepared to take a bet on it. In fact, the best they could agree on was that no one had ever heard of it happening before.

'And hey,' said the magpie, 'if it did happen, you could end up more beautiful than Satanella. AND you could probably get into the *Guinness Book of Records* too.'

In the end, no one could say anything to make Tristram feel safer about letting the crazy old witch perform magic on him, so the poor little dog shrugged his shoulders, closed his eyes and said, 'OK, get on with it, then.'

'Right,' said Gertrude. 'Go and stand over there under that tree.'

Tristram, who was now too scared to open his eyes, walked straight into the tree.

'Oww!' he cried, still refusing to open his eyes. 'You never said it would hurt like that. Am I a handsome prince now?'

'You walked into the tree,' said Gertrude. 'I haven't done the magic yet.'

'Oh.'

'Right. Now stand perfectly still,' Gertrude said, ready to cast her spell.

She shut her eyes and walked straight into the tree.

'Oww!' Gertrude cried. 'Who did that?'

The dog and the old witch opened their eyes, got themselves into the right positions and closed them again. Gertrude started wailing a weird, scary wail that made the cats' fur stand on end and all the leaves fall from the trees. There was a bright flash, a thick cloud of smoke and the smell of burnt fur.

The magpie had flown back up into the tree and was the only one who could see anything for all the smoke, though all he could see was all the smoke. A breeze turned up from somewhere and gradually blew the smoke away.

The smell of burnt fur had actually been the smell of burnt hair. Gertrude was now completely bald and it was not a pretty sight. The burnt-hair smell had hidden another smell – burnt clothes. Gertrude was also completely naked, but instead of being something that would scare the living daylights out of a blind man, she was actually quite cute in an I-Wouldn't-Mind-That-For-Dinner-With-Some-New-Potatoes-And-Apple-Sauce kind of way.

Gertrude was a piglet.

'Oink oink, oops,' she said, and began

nuzzling through the fallen leaves for slugs.

All the cats' fur seemed to be stuck standing on end, and no amount of preening and shaking could return them to normal.[27]

High up in the tree, the magpie had been out of range of Gertrude's magic and was completely unchanged.

But where was Tristram?

It took a while to find him. There were several reasons for this:

- He was very, very tiny.
- He was hiding under a leaf because . . .
- He was a mouse, which, as everyone knows, is about the favourite thing cats like to eat, apart from tiny defenceless birds.

'Double oops,' said Gertrude. 'Mind you, every cloud has a silver lining. I had no idea that slugs were so incredibly delicious.'

---

[27] *It would stay like that forever, unchanged by moulting or rain or any hair product. Each of the cats, including their future kittens, looked permanently terrified until their dying day.*

Tristram made a break for it and ran up the tree without any of the cats seeing him.

'Well, I suppose it could have been worse,' said Flapwig. 'Though I'm not quite sure how.'

'So where's the little dog?' said Gorsehinge. 'And, more to the point, *what* is the little dog?'

Only the magpie knew the answer because he had tucked Tristram safely under his wing. Magpies also like eating mice, but usually not until they are dead and have rotted a bit, so at least for now Tristram was sort of safe.

'I say, piglet lady,' the magpie called down to Gertrude, 'I'm assuming that you are still a witch and can still do magic.'

'Probably,' the old young piglet witch replied. 'There is a possibility, however, that I might have lost some of my powers, a bit, kind of.'

'So they won't be as wonderful as they were before?' said the magpie sarcastically.

'Maybe not,' said Gertrude. 'It's hard to tell. I mean, the spell I just did was the first one I've done for a while.'

'WHAT?' the magpie shouted.

'Well, I was never allowed to do magic stuff when all the family were in the drains with me, and since I've been on my own down there, there's never been much point,' Gertrude explained.

Oh God, the magpie said to himself.

The magpie knew there was no choice but for Gertrude to have another go.

'And who knows,' she said, 'now I've had a bit of practice, I might be better at it.'

Hold on to that thought, hold on to that thought, the magpie said to himself, trying really hard to believe it and failing completely.

Under the magpie's wing, Tristram was shivering and whimpering.

'Don't let the cats get me,' he whispered.

'It's all right,' the magpie reassured him. 'They don't know you're a mouse.'

Right at that moment Flapwig called up to the magpie, 'Where's the little dog? What happened to him?'

'I think he turned into an eagle,' the magpie

called back, flying off. 'Now, the piglet witch lady is going to do some more magic to try to change herself into something else, so I suggest all you cats move a long way away in case you end up even worse than you are now.'

'That's got rid of them,' he whispered to Tristram, as he flew down to Gertrude with the mouse buried in his feathers. 'OK, lady witch pig, do your magic.'

'Right, but first of all, magpie, you two fly out of range,' said Gertrude. 'This time I'll use the holistic wholemeal method.'

She closed her piggy eyes and concentrated.

The sky grew very dark above where they were standing. The cats, who were hiding behind a big bush, panicked and ran out into the forest beyond the wasteland.

A strange, weird, wailing, farty sort of noise filled the air, which was probably just a regular pig noise, and there was a very bright flash that blinded everyone.

Queen Anaglypta did not look like a queen. Unlike Mordonna – her second cousin, three-and-a-half times removed, who was devastatingly beautiful with the power to make any man swoon at her feet – Queen Anaglypta looked like a rather timid mouse in a cardigan that had been knitted for someone who was a completely different shape. She had a kindly but plain face that looked as if angry words had never come out of it. She was like a spoonful of indigestion medicine – safe, uncomplicated and soothing. Normally she smiled a lot, so everyone liked her, but today she did not.

Today Anaglypta was lost. Not just a little bit lost where she could ask a passing stranger for help, but totally and completely lost – in a very dark forest at the back of Castle Twilight. There was no one else, just her and a huge amount of darkness jammed in between thousands of trees covered in dead leaves. She hadn't been able to sit still and wait for news when Mordonna's search parties had gone off looking for her beloved son Tristram, so Anaglypta had gone out herself to look for him.

The trouble was that she had left without any sort of plan, map, guide person or dog, mobile phone or GPS, and the extra trouble was that this was the first time she had ever been to Transylvania Waters and its capital Dreary, so she didn't even know where the nearest lolly shop was, never mind which road went where.

'I am lost,' Anaglypta said.

'Yes, you are, aren't you?' said a chocolatey smooth voice from the shadows.

The forest was so dark it was impossible to see who the voice belonged to, or to know exactly where it was coming from.

Being a witch herself and coming from

Shangrila Lakes – which was a kingdom of wizards and magic like Transylvania Waters, only a lot smaller and with lower property prices on the unfashionable side of the world – the Queen knew only too well that it was impossible to tell from the tone or volume of a voice what its owner might be like. Tiny ants could sound like giants and ferocious skin-ripping carnivores could sound as small and sweet as a little baby.

So Queen Anaglypta was scared, very hugely scared.

She decided to turn back and do some very fast running away, except she hadn't the faintest idea where back or away was. Anaglypta sat down in the middle of what she assumed was the path and began to cry.

'Do not be afraid, beautiful lady,' said the voice. 'I am your friend.'

The Queen shivered.

'I am not dangerous,' said the voice. 'I am as I sound – chocolatey smooth – and I am entranced by your comely beauty.'

The Queen also knew that the most dangerous

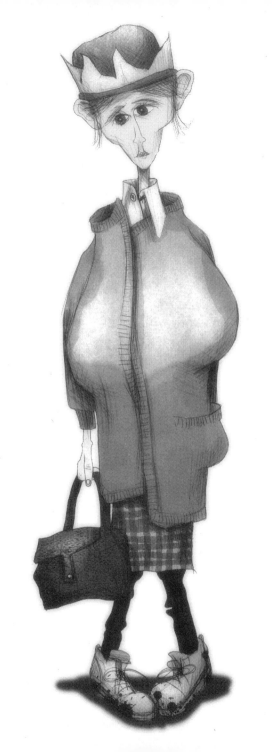

creatures were often the ones that sounded the sweetest, but it had been a very long time since anyone or anything had called her beautiful or paid her any compliment at all, and the voice did sound so very handsome and she had daydreamed of trading in her husband, the King of Shangrila Lakes, who had stopped appreciating her years ago. She had even gone as far as making a few discreet enquiries regarding the hiring of a dragon to convert her husband into a small pile of charcoal.

'If you are my friend,' she said, 'come out of the darkness so I can see you.'

And at that very moment a beam of pure moonlight shone down through the skeletal branches to where Queen Anaglypta sat, and as it did so the owner of the very handsome voice emerged from the shadows and stood before her.

He was everything the Queen would have dreamt of, if she had ever admitted to dreaming about a gorgeous young man sweeping her off her feet.[28]

---

[28] *Which she had secretly done on more than fourteen occasions.*

He was tall, but not too tall, young, but not too young, slim, but not skinny. The stranger was a perfectly formed medium-height man.

The thought *I might be old enough to be his mother, well, actually, I am old enough to be his mother. No, no, don't pretend I'm not,* tried to form inside Queen Anaglypta's head, but she barred it from entering.

The thought *Well, now he can see me up close, he's hardly going to choose me, a middle-aged mother of an unspecified number of children and, oh sod it, I am old enough to be his mother,* did enter her head, even though she tried very hard to ignore it.

'My lady,' he said, kneeling before her. 'Would that I had a broom so that I could sweep you off your feet.'

'I am off my feet,' Anaglypta replied, which was true as she was sitting on the ground. She tried to hide her face by staring into her lap, but the man with the handsome voice cupped her chin in his hands and lifted her face towards the moonlight.

'I am old enough to be your mother,' the Queen said with a great weary sigh of unhappiness.

'But, my darling,' said Handsome Voice, 'you are young enough to be my wife.'

Queen Anaglypta fainted, which, of course, was the perfect ladylike thing to do under the circumstances.

When she came to she was riding a horse, or rather, Handsome Voice was riding the horse with his arms round Anaglypta to stop her from falling off.

'Where are we going, my lord?' she said.

'Far, Far Away.'

'I have never been there, though I have heard that it's extremely beautiful.'

'As are you, my lady.'

Handsome Voice was a true royal prince and he did come from Far, Far Away, which was famous for having the most handsome princes anywhere in the whole world. His true name was Prince Forelock.

When they were some distance away, which is more than not far, but less than a long way, Prince

Forelock left the road and stopped in a small glade[29] by a stream.

'We will stop here and rest a while,' he said.

'About time too,' said his horse.

Prince Forelock reached into his saddle bag and pulled out a bacon sandwich, which he fed to the Queen. Between mouthfuls she asked him why he had come to Transylvania Waters, and he explained that his parents had sent him to woo the newly changed gorgeous witch, Satanella.

'Ah,' said Queen Anaglypta, 'Dreary is overrun with princes, counts, barons and noblemen, all with the same idea. You've no idea how quickly the news of her transformation spread across the world. Twitter was bursting at the seams with nothing else for days.'

'And all shall return home empty-handed,' said Prince Forelock. 'All except me, that is, for I have found you.'

'You seem to forget that I am a married woman,'

---

[29] *Which is not a type of furniture polish, no matter what it says on the can in the supermarket.*

Queen Anaglypta whispered, putting her hand on her noble suitor's shoulder.

As her fingers touched the red velvet of his tunic, a shiver ran through her from head to toe. Actually, the shiver didn't run. It walked very slowly and tickled every vein in her body, making her blood turn orange and start to boil.

'I suspect, my lady, that not so long ago, you were making discreet enquiries regarding the hiring of a dragon to convert your husband into a small pile of charcoal,' said the Prince.

'How on earth –?' Queen Anaglypta began.

'My family breed such dragons,' Prince Forelock said. 'It is an ancient Far, Far Away custom perfected by my distant ancestors.'

He also explained that he had fallen in love with the Queen the very instant he had seen her, immediately texting home to organise for the finest toasting-dragon in the burn[30] to be sent to bless her husband with its wonderful flames.

---

[30] *A 'burn' of dragons is like a flock of sheep, or a shoal of fish, or a complaint of teachers.*

'And, oh light of my life, I have this very moment received a text to say that your late husband is now a small pile of the finest charcoal, nestling in the bottom of two porcelain jars, one on its way to a small cave in Tristan da Cunha and the other wedged into the hull of a space probe that has just been launched to crash land on Saturn.'

'Why two jars?' asked the Queen.

'There are bad wizards in this world who would reconstitute dead people from their ashes, if the price is right. Our deluxe service divides the ashes into two parts and sends them as far away as possible from each other.'

'I should feel guilty, shouldn't I?' said the Queen. 'I know he was an awful husband, but I'm sure I should feel a bit guilty.'

'Well, no,' Prince Forelock added. 'The deluxe service also includes our finest Clear Conscience Spell.'

'Wow,' said Anaglypta. 'Well, that just leaves our age difference to worry about. Or do you have a spell for that, too?'

'Actually, I do,' the Prince said.

The pitch-black forest flashed bright white for a moment and the magic was done.

It was not, as Queen Anaglypta had thought, a spell that would make her younger, but one that made the Prince older.

Oh well, she thought. *You can't win them all.*

Prince Forelock was still tall, but not too tall, slim, but not skinny – he was a perfectly formed medium-height man. However, he now had a small,

but small-enough-to-hide-under-a-comb-over bald spot, a slight stoop, but only from certain angles, and a lot more fillings in his teeth.

But even if he had had a wooden leg, a hump, Belgian filing-clerk spectacles and a second hump covered in pimples, he would still have been a massive improvement over Husband Version One – who had had all those things with added fleas and pimples – and Queen Anaglypta would have still loved him. How could she not?

'We must hurry home to my kingdom and get you crowned King of Shangrila Lakes,' she said. 'Though I suppose we ought to get married first.'

'But what about your poor son?' Prince Forelock asked.

'Son?'

'Your poor lost little son. Should we not put our happiness aside while we search for him?' said the Prince.

'Oh, umm, yes, I suppose we should,' said the Queen. 'Though, I'm sure he's OK.'

7

Of course there was no sign of Tristram.

Everyone was running Hither and Thither, and to other strangely named places as well, looking for him, but none of them knew that he was no longer a small dog. The result was complete chaos, as more and more small dogs were grabbed, not just from Hither and Thither, but from Here and There too, and carried back to Castle Twilight in the hope of claiming a reward that was growing bigger by the hour. The castle was now surrounded by hundreds of angry dog owners demanding their pets back and threatening revolution.

Satanella was in disgrace. After all, everything had been her fault. If she hadn't been so vain and

selfish in the first place, she would have got Tristram changed into a handsome prince at the same time she had been turned into a beautiful princess. Now she had been banished to The Naughty Tower.[31]

She was locked inside with nothing to eat, except for food that would give her really bad spots. All she had to distract her was a television with only one channel to watch, and the footage streamed from a camera that had been set up in a room where all the suitors from around the world had come when they had heard about how she had been turned into an incredibly hot and perfect princess. There were dozens of suitors, ranging from drop dead gorgeous to drop dead dead with bits falling off. They all carried enormous bags of money and jewels and promises of happiness ever after, with added bacon and chocolate, and all Satanella could do was watch them from afar.

---

[31] *Which is like The Naughty Corner, with added damp and slime and no way out just by saying you're sorry.*

Meanwhile, Tristram was not locked in a tower.

Nor was he a small defenceless mouse anymore and neither was he a badger, an omelette, or a Giant Patagonian Laughing Toad. In the previous two hours he had been all these things, as Gertrude had tried over and over again to perform the right spell, and while some of the creatures had bits that he had liked,[32] none of them were exactly or even remotely what he wanted to be for the rest of his life.

Now – and this had been by accident when Gertrude had tripped over a rusty tin can that cut her leg badly releasing a terrible torrent of swear words from her mouth – Tristram was actually a fairly good-looking young man with quite a few bits that he liked very much and guessed he would like a

---

[32] *He had particularly liked the armpit smell and deep chuckle of the Patagonian Laughing Toad and the weasel's whiskers.*

lot more as he got to know them better.[33]

Each time Gertrude had changed Tristram into another life form, she herself had transformed and ended up as a small dog that looked quite a bit like the dog Tristram had been, except she was a girl dog, not a boy dog. This, of course, led to quite a lot of 'oh-how-we-laughed' hilarity when the search parties looking for Tristram as a dog kept getting very excited when they came across Gertrude. The hilarity and excitement only lasted for a short time and was followed by misery, confusion and dampness when Gertrude cast a nasty spell on them that made them keep rushing to the lavatory every ten minutes, made worse by the fact that it should have been every five minutes.

Gertrude had quite liked being a dog, but the endless 'rescues' got too much so she changed herself again.

'This,' she said as she flew up into the tree where the magpie was sitting, 'is the last time I'm doing this.'

---

[33] *Thumbs, for example.*

'Hello, gorgeous,' said the magpie. 'What's a pretty little thing like you doing out in the dark forest?'

Gertrude had two options: change herself into something that wasn't a magpie or shrug her wings and live happily ever after. And she had to admit, now that she had a magpie's brain, the magpie did look rather handsome.

OK, she said to herself, *I'll give happily ever after a go. I can always change into something else if it doesn't work.*

At that precise moment Crown Prince Tristram Jolyon De-Vere Creak walked directly beneath the branch the two magpies were sitting on, both of them quite unaware of who he was because Gertrude had kept her eyes shut tight after her first two transformation spells had gone so badly wrong.

Barely a mile ahead of Tristam in the very dark forest – which seemed to be getting darker by the minute due to the fact that night was falling – his mother and Prince Forelock were riding round and round in circles looking for him.

I wonder which way leads back to the castle, Tristram said to himself.

If he had only thought to say it out loud, the two magpies could have told him, but he hadn't so they didn't. And if he had said it out loud, they might have realised who he was, instead of mistaking him for yet another prince coming to woo Satanella. And if he had had sharper hearing, he would have heard the magpies say to each other, 'Look at that idiot walking round and round in circles down there,' and he would've told them who he really was.

The circles that Tristram were walking in and the circles his mother and Prince Forelock were riding in kept crossing, so it was only going to be a matter of time until they bumped into each other.

Night fell even lower and, as it did so, it became colder and colder and the circle-walkers also got colder and colder.

I think I will bury myself in some leaves and wait until morning, Tristram thought.

'Maybe we should bury ourselves in some leaves

and wait until morning,' said Queen Anaglypta.[34]

'Yeah thanks, great,' said Prince Forelock's horse. 'And I suppose I just have to stand here and freeze all night.'

Prince Forelock, who had never buried himself in any plant materials, alive or dead, agreed with the horse.

'I think we should make our way back to Dreary and find an inn for the night,' he said.

Queen Anaglypta didn't like the idea in case Forelock caught sight of Satanella and dumped the Queen in exchange for the Flood princess, but he assured her that there was no one in any galaxy who he would rather be with than Queen Anaglypta.

So they turned and rode in the direction they thought was the right way to town.

---

[34] *The De-Vere Creaks were well-known for burying themselves in leaves on a regular basis. In fact, there was an annual Mulching Festival in Shangrila Lakes, where the entire population buried themselves in rotting foliage for up to thirteen days to celebrate the leaves falling off the trees every autumn. 'Why else would the leaves fall off, if not so that we could bury ourselves in them?' everyone said.*

It wasn't.

But it didn't matter because the horse tripped over a lump buried under some leaves and sprained its ankle. Queen Anaglypta and Prince Forelock had no choice but to snuggle into the leaves, which were not only damp and smelly but actually colder than the air around them.

The lump they had tripped over was, of course, Tristram, who swore loudly and complained that even in the middle of a dark impenetrable forest a person couldn't get a decent sleep without some clumsy great horse tripping over him.

'I recognise that voice,' said Queen Anaglypta, not realising that the young man who now stood before her was her own son, who she had only ever known as a small dog. 'Now, where have I heard it before?'

I recognise that voice, Tristram muttered to himself. *Mother.*

Interregnum – Act 1

INTERIOR CASTLE TWILIGHT —
THE BACON LOUNGE[35]

MORDONNA, Queen of Transylvania Waters, paces up and down in front of the window. NERLIN, King of Transylvania Waters, sits in a crumbly old armchair.

                    MORDONNA
This has all gone too far. These books are supposed to be the chronicles of the Starship *Enterprise*. No, no, I mean the chronicles of the incredible Flood family. And several thousand words have passed with barely a mention of our wonderfulness and incredibleness. I mean,

---

[35] *This is the Standard Bacon Lounge as opposed to the Crispy Bacon Lounge, which is in a completely different place. I know this is probably obvious, but I feel it needs saying.*

who wants to read about cats
and magpies?

NERLIN
Indeed, my darling, and who
cares if some stupid little
dog has gone missing?

Mordonna looks around to make sure
no one is within earshot.

MORDONNA
You're quite right. Inviting
the Creaks here was a big
mistake. I know they're our
relatives and all that, but
they're very common. I think
we both agree that Satanella
did the right thing in the
end, insisting I didn't
change Tristram into a
handsome prince. The two of
them might have got married
and could have even ended
up as King and Queen of our
wonderful kingdom. Then what
would people think?

NERLIN
People, what people?

MORDONNA
I don't know. You know,
people.

NERLIN
I never realised you were such
a snob, but then I suppose
you are a royal princess and
just about the absolutely
top witch anywhere, ever.

MORDONNA
It's got nothing to do with
being a snob. It's that
the people of Transylvania
Waters, our loyal subjects,
deserve nothing but the best
and the Creaks are not the
best.

NERLIN
Second best?

MORDONNA

No, not even that. We, the
Floods, are the best, the
second best and the third
best. We win gold, silver
and bronze.

Nerlin rises and nods in agreement.

MORDONNA (CONT'D)

Exactly. So now we've got
that sorted out, let's have
no more talk about magpies,
stupid little cats and dogs,
and sub-standard relations,
and get back to the important
story — which, of course, is
us.

After the interregnum[36] Mordonna and Nerlin needed a cup of tea and a special biscuit because, as everyone knows, interregnums can be pretty exhausting, so exhausting, in fact, that the King and Queen both needed two of the Very Special Biscuits.[37]

'As I was saying,' Nerlin continued, 'before this dog-changing-into-human fiasco and all the trouble it has stirred up, I've had enough of being King and I want to retire. I want to go high up into the mountains to the Enchanted Valley of the Impossible Waterfall,[38] and build a little cottage by the river for

---

[36] *Oh for goodness sake, look it up in a dictionary.*

[37] *See the back of this book for more information, though, of course, you can't see the recipe.*

[38] *See* The Floods 12: Bewitched.

the two of us, and keep chickens and ducks and quail and do gardening and watch the birds, so long as none of them are magpies.'

'Couldn't we just build the cottage and use it as a weekender?' Mordonna suggested. 'Then you'd have the best of both worlds. You'd still be King during the week doing all the ruling stuff, but each weekend you could potter about at the cottage.'

'I suppose it would do for a start,' said Nerlin.

'Except for the hassle of travelling up there and back every week.'

'I'm sure Winchflat can come up with something to sort that out,' said Mordonna. 'Maybe like that transporter device they have in *Star Trek*.'

Nerlin pointed out that *Star Trek* was all made up and machines like that didn't actually exist. Mordonna said she knew that, but Winchflat was a genius and if anyone could make a transporter that could dissolve you in one place and join all the bits of you back together again in another, then surely he could.

'Maybe,' Nerlin agreed. 'But it could take years for him to make it. I want to retire now.'

Mordonna tried persuading Nerlin to have his cottage in one of the banqueting halls of Castle Twilight.

'After all,' she said, 'there are several rooms that are big enough for a cottage with a pond and a chicken run and potted trees round the walls. It would feel just like being outdoors.'

'That's ridiculous,' said Nerlin.

He wasn't sure why, but he refused to have an 'indoor outdoors', even if the ceiling was painted to look like the sky and Winchflat made a special cloud machine to make it rain inside whenever they wanted.

So it was decided that Nerlin and Mordonna would organise for a cottage to be built up in the Enchanted Valley, and while Winchflat was working on the transporter, they would fly up and down on turbo-charged broomsticks (currently the fastest way to travel, though they did tend to make your eyes bleed).

'And when Winchflat has perfected a trans-porter, you can start using that,' said Mordonna.

'I'm not so sure,' said Nerlin. 'I don't want bits of me ending up in different places from each other. I mean, my feet could end up in Tristan da Cunha and my bottom in a caravan by the Belgium seaside, and then I wouldn't be able to go to the lavatory and I would explode.'

'Don't be silly,' said Mordonna. 'Of course, we wouldn't use it until it's been thoroughly tested

first. We'll start off transporting some sheep, and if that turns out OK then we'll transport some Belgian Traffic Wardens, and if that turns out OK we'll try normal people, and if that turns OK, well, then you can use it.'

'I don't want a load of sheep and traffic wardens up in the Enchanted Valley at my wonderful cottage eating all my lovely flowers and baby ducks,' said Nerlin.[39]

Mordonna suggested that they get their children to take it in turns standing in for Nerlin as ruler each weekend while he was at the cottage.

'That way,' she said, 'we can try them all out and, who knows, maybe one of them will actually like it and want to take over the job permanently?'

---

[39] *And just to stop your worries and your imaginations from getting all stressed out, I can reveal that none of the above actually ended up at Nerlin's beautiful cottage, though there were a few bottoms that got mixed up. But, hey, you've never seen anything as funny as a Belgian Traffic Warden with a sheep's bottom all covered in wool. Though at least the traffic wardens had the materials to knit themselves nice warm scarves.*

'Brilliant,' said Nerlin, and went off to look for Winchflat.

Winchflat was in his Number Seven Laboratory, where he worked on inventions that contained bacon.[40] This was always the first place anyone looking for him went to, not just because he spent more time in there than any of his other twelve laboratories, but because some of the other ones were top-secret, invisible or dangerous, or all three. And anyway, Number Seven Laboratory smelled so much better than the rest.

When Nerlin told Winchflat that he wanted a *Star Trek*-type transporter machine to go up to his

---

[40] *And believe me, there were a lot of them. Though, to tell the truth, most of the inventions didn't actually need the bacon and some would have probably worked better without it, but hey, BACON!!*

cottage, his son was delighted.

'I often thought about trying to make a machine like that,' Winchflat said, 'but because it would take so much time and work, I've never got round to it. Now I've got a reason to. Brilliant!'

What he didn't tell his father was that he had been working on a transporter since the age of seven, but had had mixed success and finally got bored with it, which was his way of telling himself that something was too difficult to do. Winchflat could never admit to himself or to anyone else that there might actually be an invention he couldn't invent.

He had previously had some minor success with transporting solid objects from A to B, but it had mostly involved getting small pieces of bacon to de-materialise from his plate and re-materialise in his mouth.

So it can't be impossible, he told himself. Winchflat soon discovered that there was more to it than just enlarging everything, when the bigger version had transported a very angry fat duck into his mouth. It had taken two weeks to get the taste

of what that duck had done in his mouth out of his mouth, even after he had scrubbed his tongue with steel wool dipped in bleach.[41]

For Winchflat's next attempt he made sure to keep his mouth shut and stuck cotton buds up his nose.[42] This time he also made sure the duck was wearing a nappy. But of course that created another problem because he forgot to weigh the nappy and, as everyone knows, when you transport ANYTHING from ANYWHERE to SOMEWHERE ELSE it is VERY IMPORTANT to maintain the EXACT TOTAL weight of whatever it is you are transporting. If you don't, various things could happen:

---

[41] *I know I don't need to say this, but I have been told to for legal reasons – DON'T TRY THIS AT HOME (or ANYWHERE ELSE).*

[42] *See footnote 41. Which reminds me, when my cousin Stephen and I were kids, we persuaded his little sister to see how many daisies she could stuff up her nose. She ended up at the doctor's, where the daisies had to be pulled out with tweezers. We never did find out exactly how many she had got up there, but I bet she would have got into the* Guinness Book of Records.

1. Everything will get transported OK but not as far as you planned, and there is no way of knowing where it has gone unless you had transported a person with a mobile phone.

2. Everything will be transported to exactly where you wanted it to go, but bits of it will be missing.[43]

3. Everything will be transported to exactly where you wanted it to go, but everything will be smaller so it will become the same weight as when you first entered it into the transporter.[44]

4. Everything will be transported to a potato farm in Belgium.

5. Everything will turn inside out, which doesn't bear thinking about.

---

[43] *No one has discovered where these missing bits actually went.*

[44] *Making it a MASSIVELY successful weight-loss machine in the future, once all the wrinkles have been ironed out – wrinkles in the design and build of the machine, and wrinkles left on fat people who have lost the weight.*

Winchflat's duck suddenly vanished and reappeared in a cupboard under the stairs of a house in Tristan da Cunha, which was really weird because none of the buildings there have staircases.

'Oh well,' Winchflat said, and tried again.

This time he used a chicken, which ended up on the duck's back. It was at this point Winchflat decided that his transporter needed a reverse gear, a sort of undo button that could bring whatever had been sent off into the wide blue wherever back again.[45]

Nerlin sent out for a box of Royal Crayons and a Royal Sketchbook and sat down to design his retirement cottage. Nerlin had a hard enough time drawing conclusions, never mind pictures. He had never ever in his whole life tried to draw one, not even something as simple as a ball. Growing up in the damp drains beneath Dreary, it had been difficult to draw. Rats ate the crayons, and the paper grew mould that could kill penicillin. Not that Nerlin had wanted to be an artist, but now he felt creative urges

---

[45] *Or, in the case of the duck and the chicken, not so much wide and blue, as narrow and dark.*

stirring in a tiny room at the back of his brain.

Not only would I end up living in a lovely cottage in the Enchanted Valley, Nerlin said to himself, *it would be a cottage I would have designed all by myself.*

Like most things in life, the more you do something, the easier it gets. In less than a week, Nerlin had learnt that the pointy end of the crayon was the one you drew with and that to open a sketchbook you had to turn over the pages. He also discovered that a red crayon was different from a blue one, and that neither of them tasted as nice as an orange one.

Nerlin shut his eyes and tried to imagine his dream cottage. He had no problems thinking of descriptions like '*thatched roof*', '*roses round the door*', '*self-closing toilet seat*' and '*bacon library*', and he could see these inside his head perfectly, but when he opened his eyes and tried to draw them, everything went wiggly and came out wrong. So he tried to start off with something simple.

'When I go to live in the cottage,' Nerlin said, 'I will have a dog. I might even have two, and we will all play together.

'And,' he continued, 'we will play with a red rubber ball.'

So he closed his eyes again and there in his head was a beautiful big red rubber ball. It lay in the grass with the sunlight reflecting off its lovely coat of dog dribble.

Nerlin opened his eyes and began to draw.

A simple red rubber ball – no grass, no dog dribble, nothing difficult. What could possibly go wrong?

Except his red ball was blue.

And it was square.

Nerlin was depressed.

'I can't even draw something as simple as a red rubber ball,' he complained.

'You can't be good at everything, my darling,' Mordonna said. 'You are the King of the greatest country in the world. You are the world's top wizard.[46] You don't need to be able to draw. There are other people who can do that for you.'

---

[46] *As we have seen in earlier Floods books, Nerlin was actually a pretty rubbish wizard, but everyone loved him, so they didn't care.*

'But I want to live in a cottage I designed all by myself,' Nerlin said.

'And so you shall, my beloved,' Mordonna replied. 'We will use one of Winchflat's Magic Hats.'

Over the years Winchflat had developed magic hats for hundreds of different occasions, including some that were programmed to do almost anything.[47]

'Winchflat will fit you with a Magic Hat that will take the pictures inside your head and turn them into a drawing that will be exactly the same,' said Mordonna.

'Oh sure, no problem,' said Winchflat.

He sat his father down, strapped the hat – which was more like a strange crash-helmet – on his head, plugged it into an electric socket and turned it on.[48] Winchflat then adjusted the controls until Nerlin's ears, which were poking out of holes on each side of the hat, turned a lovely shade of blue. He consulted a colour chart and fine-tuned the colour until it was exactly right.

'Now, Father,' he said, 'I want you to start

---

[47] *See the back of this book for a selection of Winchflat's Magic Hats, including one that might be a bit rude and another one that will be VERY RUDE, if I can distract my publisher long enough to get away with it.*

[48] *Yes, once again, see footnote 41. In fact, let's just say, don't try ANYTHING in this book ANYWHERE.*

imagining your cottage. Start at the front gate, walk up the garden path and into the house. Go through each room and imagine every little detail, right down to the colour of the toilet paper and how many pairs of dirty underpants there are in the laundry basket.'

Nerlin's ears began to throb in waves of different colours, and as they did so a robot arm began to draw on a huge sheet of paper Winchflat had pinned up on the wall.

It was an amazing thing to see. If Nerlin changed his mind, another robot arm rubbed out the bits he didn't like.

When the ground floor was finished, Nerlin thought about the upstairs with wonderful bathrooms, and bedrooms with balconies that overlooked perfect views. There was even a dog's bedroom with wallpaper covered in pictures of squeaky toys and special dog cake. Nerlin and Mordonna didn't actually have a pet dog, but they both knew that no country cottage was complete without one.

'And anyway,' Nerlin said, 'even if we don't

get a dog, we could end up with some naughty grandchildren who could sleep there.'

'Absolutely,' Mordonna agreed. 'And if they are really horrible children, I could change them into dogs with a special spell.'

'You miss Satanella being a dog, don't you?'

'Yes,' Mordonna said. 'Now that she's a young woman, it's not quite the same going through her hair for ticks and fleas.'

Once the upstairs was finished, Nerlin imagined the cellars and the robot arm drew them too. Winchflat was particularly interested in this part of the cottage and quite a few of his creative suggestions were added to the plans, including many exciting innovations that Nerlin had never heard of and some he wished he had never heard of.[49]

Finally there was the garden to design and here Nerlin got a bit carried away. There were sunflowers as tall as houses with centres the size of twenty

---

[49] *And no, DO NOT turn to the back of the book to look for them. These are the sort of things that only wizards are allowed to see.*

dinner plates, and roses so large you could climb inside them and go to sleep, and leaves made of chocolate. This meant that Winchflat had to build a special machine to make these plants because they didn't really exist. There was also special grass that never needed mowing and a crystal-clear stream with bacon-flavoured fish.

Mordonna said they had to do everything properly so that they could submit the plans to the council and get building approval.

'What's the point of that?' Nerlin asked.

'Well, we don't want some petty official coming along later and telling us the whole thing has to be pulled down because it doesn't comply with the regulations,' Mordonna explained.

'That's not going to happen,' said Nerlin.

'How can you be so sure?' Mordonna replied. 'You know what office people can be like. And yes, Transylvania Waters is the greatest and most magical kingdom anywhere, but council officials are the same all over the world. They want everyone to think they're important.'

'No, won't happen.'

'How do you know?' Mordonna asked.

'Because I am Transylvania Waters's Head of Planning,' said Nerlin with a big grin, 'and I give myself full permission to build my cottage. In fact, I will even give myself a grant to go out and buy everything I need.'

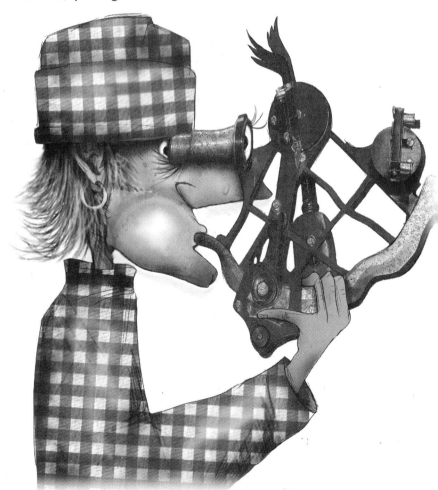

9

The cottage and garden were created and built exactly how Nerlin had imagined them, except the cottage wasn't made of gingerbread and cake because the builders kept eating it. So they changed over to more conventional materials like bricks and cement, though it took a few days for the builders to realise this, by which time most of them had lost a lot of teeth.

'They should change the bakery,' the builders had complained. 'These roof tiles are as hard as slate. They're almost inedible.'

But finally the cottage was finished, and Mordonna and Nerlin called a family meeting to tell the children what was happening.

'So every weekend your father and I will be going up to the cottage and one of you will be left in charge,' Mordonna told them.

'What, you mean a sort of time-share king?' said Valla.

'Or queen,' Betty added.

'Yes, from Friday night until Sunday night,' said Nerlin.

'Can we make laws and stuff like that?' the twins asked.

'Oh, I'm not sure about that,' said Mordonna.

'So we won't be real kings and queens then?' said Betty. 'More like house-sitters?'

'Umm, er . . .' said Nerlin.

'Why on earth would any of us want to do that?' said Valla. 'It'd be kind of like feeding the dogs while you two skived off every weekend.'

'Maybe they could make laws that were only laws when it was their particular turn to be in charge,' Nerlin suggested to Mordonna, seeing the promise of his lovely weekends up in paradise ebbing away.

This made Nerlin slip off into a wonderful

daydream that involved him and Mordonna swimming underneath the Impossible Waterfall[50] and eating bacon sandwiches with lots of barbecue sauce running down their chins while brilliantly coloured skylarks flew above them singing saucy songs.[51]

The next thing Nerlin knew, Mordonna was shaking him awake and telling him it had been agreed that the children could make one new law every month, but if she or Nerlin thought it was a bad law they could abolish it when they got back. So the worst that could happen was Transylvania Waters would have a bad law for one weekend.

A set of guidelines was drawn up that each law had to follow:

- No animals are to be hurt or embarrassed. (Except for cats, which are really evil and deserve everything they get.)
- Any law that incorporates bacon and/or

[50] See The Floods 12: Bewitched.

[51] The saucy songs are not rude songs but songs about sauces, like the aforementioned barbecue sauce.

chocolate will score an extra fifty points.

- Any law that includes the destruction of bagpipes will score an extra one hundred points.
- Guidelines and rules will be added and/or deleted as and when King Nerlin feels like it.
- No declaring war on any other country – even Belgium.
- No entering the Eurovision Song Contest while the King's back is turned.
- No tartan.
- Or Vegemite.
- Or goldfish juggling.
- Or guide lines or scout lines or lines of guides or lines of scouts or broccoli.
- Use-by dates must be printed in very, very small blurry writing.
- No tearing along the dotted line – just walk slowly.
- No.
- Or not.

Most of the guidelines made no sense at all, and that suited everyone because it meant they could be ignored. All except the last rule:

• No ignoring the guidelines.

Then, of course, there was the problem of deciding who should be King or Queen first. Everyone and no one wanted to go and sometimes at the same time. Obvious choices like going from eldest down to youngest or going in alphabetical order were quickly rejected for being too humanlike and boring. Putting names in a hat and pulling them out was no good either because everyone was a wizard or witch and could change the writing on the bits of paper with a very simple spell. It was the same with picking the shortest or longest straw.

In the end, Mordonna waved her hands around really, really fast and pointed her finger, and whoever was nearest was it. For the next weekend, the previous weekend's 'winner' was allowed to leave the room until Mordonna had chosen, but they would have to go back in the week after, which meant that the same person could end up having to be in charge every second week.

'That's not fair,' Betty complained, but a tiny thought had begun to nag at the back of her brain. If she did become Queen, no one would ever be allowed to tell her what to do – even her mother. Betty started to believe this might actually be quite a good idea, after all. But she didn't want to give her mother the satisfaction.

'And what fantasy land have you been living in, where they told you life was fair?' Mordonna replied.

'But . . .' Betty began.

'Right, madam,' said Mordonna, pointing her finger. 'You can go first.'

Mordonna was amazed at how many swear words her youngest daughter knew. They just poured out of her, thousands upon thousands, until Mordonna began to wonder if many of them were just made up as Betty went along.[52]

'. . . PLUGOOZE!!' Betty shouted and stormed out.

'I won't let Mum get away with it,' Betty said to her best friend, Ffiona, when they were sitting back in her room. 'I'm going to make some really gross law with poo in it.'

'Oooh, what are you going to do?' Ffiona asked.

'I don't know,' said Betty. 'Let's try to think of something that will really annoy everyone.'

---

[52] *See the back of this book to read and learn a selection of Betty's brilliant swear words, some of which have already appeared in the* Floodsopedia. *It is a little-known fact that one of Betty's main hobbies is collecting disgusting things, including swear words, which she finds in interesting places such as sewers and rubbish tips. I would love to produce a book of Betty's most disgusting collections but, of course, I will never be allowed to. I know it's a terrible shame that you will never get to read about them. All I can say is, use your most disgusting imaginations.*

'But then everyone will hate you,' said Ffiona. 'Not only that, they'll feel sorry for your parents and like them even more.'

'Oh yeah, I hadn't thought of that,' said Betty. 'Still, it's only Monday. We've got until Friday to think of something.'

'So if you're only in charge for two days,' said Ffiona, 'how is everyone going to find out about the new law before the next week?'

That was when the penny dropped. In fact, a whole bagful of pennies and dolors[53] came crashing down.

Mordonna had tricked them all. She knew full well that by the time anyone heard about any new law, even if it was made on a Friday evening, the weekend would soon be over and she and Nerlin would be back in charge and could delete the new law if they wanted to. But instead of making Betty feel like her mother had won, it had just made the idea of becoming Queen more appealing.

---

[53] *'Dolors' and 'scents' are the Transylvania Waters equivalent of dollars and cents.*

So Betty and Ffiona decided to go to the Inspiration Rock, which was a big rock in the forest just out of town. No one knew why it was called the Inspiration Rock, but that had been its name for as long as anyone could remember. In fact, it had been called that long before anyone could remember, even longer than Granny Crochet, who could recall hundreds of things from three or four hundred years before she'd been born. Anyone who had a problem they couldn't find a solution to would go to the rock, pull their undies down and press their bare bottom against it in the hope of getting some inspiration.[54]

---

[54] *One of the most popular books in Transylvania Waters was* Ninety-Nine Bottoms *– the only book to have ever been banned in the kingdom. It had ninety-nine candid photos of bare bottoms being pressed against Inspiration Rock. When the book had first been published, there had been hundreds of letters sent to the* Dreary Times *from readers trying to guess who the bottoms belonged to. The book had not been banned because it was rude, but because everyone had got so fed up with the endless letters and guesses with no way of knowing who any particular bottom belonged to, except for Grenoble St Aubergine's, which had a bunch of brussels sprouts tattooed on the left buttock.*

There was also a photo of Saucy McPhoarr's bottom, which had the lines of a noughts and crosses game, and he (or she – no

'Maybe it will give us ideas on the best way to deal with Mother,' said Betty.

Ffiona wasn't so sure, but the Inspiration Rock was one of the places her mother had banned her from visiting. Mordonna had tried to ban Betty too, which made her think it must have some awesome powers her mother couldn't control.

The Inspiration Rock did possess some magical powers, because if anyone pressed their bottom against it and kept their knickers on, they would break out in dozens of big, purple, throbbing pimples. You also had to keep your eyes wide open, otherwise all your hair would fall out. If you walked round Dreary any day of the week, you would be sure to see at least one bald person hobbling around with an obviously painful pimply bottom.

Whether the Inspiration Rock actually did have magical powers that could help you, no one was really sure. Some people swore by it. Some people swore at it. There was no doubt, though, that

---

one was sure) was only too happy to let people mark the grid with a big red lipstick.

136

nothing concentrated your thoughts like pushing your bare bottom against a big rock worn smooth by thousands of other bottoms, while keeping your eyes wide open and trying to avoid the stares of complete strangers.[55]

Amazingly, for the first time in years, the rock was absolutely deserted by the time Betty and Ffiona got there. This was such a rare occurrence that Betty was instantly suspicious.

Although neither girl had ever been to the Inspiration Rock, like everyone in Transylvania Waters, they knew all about it.

'I thought it was supposed to be constantly busy, even in the middle of the night,' Ffiona said.

'It is,' said Betty. 'Something's not right.'

'So are you going to do it or not?' said Ffiona.

Betty wasn't sure. Her first thought was that her mother had been up to something. It was the sort of thing Mordonna would do and she was certainly powerful enough. Betty's second thought

---

[55] *Sometimes there were so many people seeking inspiration at the rock that there was a queue.*

137

was that the rock they were looking at wasn't the real, genuine, actual Inspiration Rock and that they had been misled. Of course, that could be a trick of Mordonna's too. Or it could simply be that the girls had taken a wrong turn in the forest.

'I suppose the only thing we can do,' said Betty, 'is try it out.'

'I don't want to,' said Ffiona, more out of shyness than anything else.

So Betty turned around and cautiously stepped backwards until her bare bottom was a few millimetres from the rock. As she touched it, there was a flash of light. It seemed to come from everywhere and was followed by a loud crash as the Inspiration Rock split right in two.

Betty, unharmed but shaken, jumped forward and pulled her undies back up.

'So, you're finally here,' said a voice from the bushes. 'I knew you would come.'

The voice was followed by a person or, to be precise, a bundle of rags shedding bits of itself as it moved. There was a smell that seemed even

more desperate than the rags and which shed itself everywhere, especially up Betty's and Ffiona's noses.

It was Gertrude Flood. Fortunately, her magic had begun to work a bit better and she'd managed to change herself back into something that was close to a human-witch-sort-of-person, apart from the two small cauliflowers where her ears should have been.

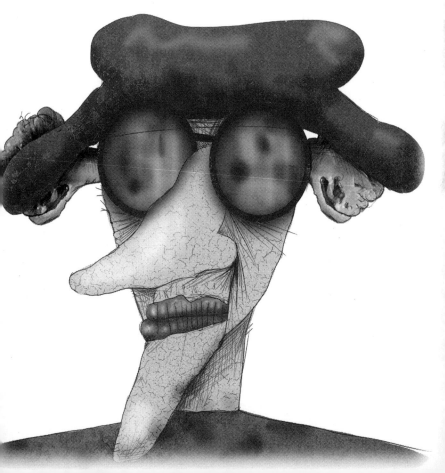

The cauliflowers were a small price to pay for not having to spend the future as Mrs Magpie.

'Hello,' she said, shaking off the last bits of rag.

As the figure straightened up, the two girls could see someone that looked remarkably like Betty's father, Nerlin.

'Dad? What on earth's happened to you?' Betty cried.

'Nothing,' said Gertrude. 'And I am not your father. In fact, I haven't seen him for years.'

She explained that she was not some really ancient distant relative of the Floods – as the cats and others had thought – but something much closer. She was Betty's aunt, Nerlin's twin sister. All the rags and smells had merely been a disguise.

'When your mother fell into the drain all those years ago and landed on your father, the rest of us hid in the deepest drains, as far away from your mother's father as possible,' Gertrude explained. 'He was livid with rage and spent months dropping bombs and deadly gas cylinders into our tunnels. A lot of us didn't survive.

'And then, a few years later,' she continued, 'when you all came back and reclaimed the throne, most of us were overjoyed and left the drains for the world above. There were only two of us who thought it might be a trap and refused to leave.'

'Two?' said Betty.

'Yes. Me and Mad Boggit,' said Gertrude. 'As far as I know, she's still down there. She found a doorway in one of the deepest tunnels and went through it and down some stairs into total darkness. I dared not follow her and she never came back, so we have no way of knowing if she is dead or alive, or both, or something else completely. I used to hear strange wailing noises that sounded like they came from a whale, but they stopped a few years ago.'

'So what made you finally leave the drains?' said Betty.

She wanted to say 'auntie', but was too shy. Betty had never said it before and it seemed like a nice thing to do. And if Gertrude could read Betty's mind – which she could – she would tell her that it would be quite nice to be called auntie.

'My spies told me there was no longer any danger. The damp was also beginning to seep into my bones,' Gertrude explained. 'It took a long time to re-adjust here. The last time I came up, the light was so bright it blinded me, but I gradually got used to it and now I'm up here for good.'

'Does my mother know about you?' Betty asked.

'I don't know,' said Gertrude. 'That depends on whether your father ever told her.'

'Neither of them has ever mentioned you,' said Betty.

And this was true. Mordonna didn't even know that Gertrude existed due to it being a Deep Dark Secret, which meant that Nerlin had NEVER told her.[56]

---

[56] *Sometimes, on deep dark winter nights when icicles hung from Castle Twilight's battlements, Nerlin would wake up shaking from a dream in which Gertrude came marching into the castle to claim the throne and throw him into the dampest, darkest dungeon. Nerlin prayed and hoped that his sister was dead so that the secret could remain buried forever. He told himself that all those years in the damp darkness must have had taken their*

As mentioned before, kings and queens in the world of wizards are not the same in the world of humans. Witches and wizards are much fairer. It is always the oldest child who becomes the next ruler, and whether they are a witch or a wizard makes no difference at all.

And so Betty discovered Nerlin's Deep Dark Secret: Gertrude was older than her twin brother – seven hours, seven minutes and seven seconds older. Which meant that:

Gertrude was the rightful ruler of Transylvania Waters, NOT Nerlin.

'Well, well, well,' said Betty with a smile. 'This is brilliant news.'

'Why?' said Ffiona and Gertrude.

'Because I will go and tell my mother, and if she ever tries to do anything I don't like, I will tell the whole world and get Mother and Father thrown into

---

toll by now and that Gertude had succumbed to some terrible damp darkness disease. In fact, Gertrude was in better health than her brother and all that had happened while she was down there was that she had grown webbed feet.

the dungeons,' Betty explained.

'But I don't want to be Queen of Transylvania Waters,' said Gertrude. 'I just want a nice quiet life in a nice little cottage by a nice peaceful stream in some nice faraway valley high up in the mountains.'

'Mother doesn't know that,' said Betty. 'And as for the cottage, I think I know the perfect place for you. Provided, of course, we can come to an arrangement . . .'

Betty would pretend that Gertrude had returned to claim the throne from Nerlin, which would drive Mordonna crazy. Initially Mordonna would assume that Gertrude's magic was as low-grade and useless as her twin brother's, so Mordonna would think dealing with Gertrude wouldn't be a problem.

Now, although Gertrude's magic was rusty, as she had shown when she had tried to help Tristram, hers was the most powerful magic in the whole of Transylvania Waters. There were spells that she alone could do, spells that had vanished into legend, where they had become mythical and hardly anyone actually believed they were real. All Gertrude needed to do was practise a bit to get her magic working correctly again.

'I just need to concentrate and focus, and concentrate, and probably concentrate and focus,' she said. 'And practise.'

'Right,' said Betty, wondering if her aunt really was the ultimate-power witch or just as useless as her dad.

'First of all,' Gertrude said, 'I'll mend the Inspiration Rock.'

She put a hand on each of the two broken halves of the rock and concentrated. There was a little flash of light and . . .

'A bowl of raspberries,' said Betty. 'Brilliant.'

'Don't panic,' said Gertrude. 'Fortunately, I do have one fantastic thing that no other wizard has got – an Undo Button.'

She explained that when Great, Great, Great plus twenty-seven more Greats Grandfather Flood, the last of the Ultimate Super-Wizards, had decided to pass his massive magical powers to one of his descendants before he died, he had chosen Gertrude. And because the magic was so powerful, he had given her an Undo Button, just in case she accidentally destroyed an entire planet or turned the whole population of the world into Belgian cabbage farmers. This invisible secret button was located in the middle of her forehead and was about the size of a ten-cent piece.

So Gertrude put one hand on the bowl of fruit, the middle finger of her other hand in the middle of her forehead and whispered a strange incantation until the bowl turned into something else.

'Oh,' said Ffiona, 'they're gorgeous.'

'Yeah,' said Betty. 'A basket of puppies.'

'Hold on, hold on,' said Gertrude, and changed the basket of puppies into an enormous pair of beige knickers. 'Wait, wait, I got the words muddled up. It's been a very long time since I've used them. I've got it now.'

Finally, the two halves of the Inspiration Rock reappeared. After one more try, the two halves became one.

The Inspiration Rock was restored.

'I think I need a bit more practice,' said Gertrude. 'Follow me.'

She led the two girls deep into the forest until they came to an ancient castle in ruins. In the middle of the castle, almost but not quite completely buried under a tangle of vines and tree roots, was a small cave. The perfect hiding place.

'This is a secret tunnel that goes down into the drains where your father and I grew up,' Gertrude said. 'I only discovered it a few months ago and you two are the only other people who know about it.'

'I don't think you need to worry about that, auntie,' said Betty. 'I'm pretty sure neither of us has the slightest desire to go down there.'

It was agreed that the two girls would go back to Castle Twilight and Betty would tell Mordonna about Gertrude's plans to claim the kingdom, and while they were gone Gertrude would practise her magic until it was restored to its full power and glory.

'So I'll see you back here tomorrow,' Gertrude said, turning her shoes into two bowls of porridge.

'You don't think maybe one day's not quite long enough?' said Betty.

'Mmm, you're probably right,' said Gertrude, turning the two bowls of porridge into two buckets of eels, which she eventually managed to turn back into a pair of shoes, even though they were on the wrong feet.

'Have you got a minute, Mother?' said Betty.

Mordonna was packing for her and Nerlin's first weekend at the retirement cottage.

'Not now, dear,' Mordonna replied. 'You know we're just about to leave.'

'I do, Mother,' Betty said as sweetly as she could. 'And I've got a word that you can take with you.'

'A word? What do you mean?'

'I've got a word, a single little eight-letter word I'd like you to put in your head for you and Daddy to talk about while you're away,' said Betty.

'One word?' said Mordonna. 'Well, that's hardly going to take up the whole weekend, is it?'

'Oh, I think it will,' said Betty.

'OK, I give up,' said Mordonna. 'Tell me the word.'

'Gertrude.'

'Gertrude? What's so special about that?' said Mordonna. 'It's just an old-lady name.'

So Daddy obviously hasn't told her, Betty thought.

'Just ask Daddy,' Betty said. 'He will tell you who the old-lady name belongs to, and do make sure you tell him that I said "belongs to" and not "belonged to".'

'What on earth are you playing at, young lady?' Mordonna snapped.

'Just ask Daddy about Gertrude,' said Betty, and made a hasty retreat as Mordonna shouted after her to come back and explain.

Mordonna told herself it was just Betty playing her usual power games like all teenage daughters do, but an uneasy feeling began to poke her in the back of the brain. She finished packing and followed the servant down to the courtyard, where Nerlin was waiting, jumping up and down with excitement like

a little boy. Mordonna tried to forget the word, but it kept tickling her thoughts and wouldn't go away.

'I can't believe we're finally going up to the Enchanted Valley to our beautiful cottage,' Nerlin said.

As Mordonna and Nerlin climbed into their brand new Going-Away-For-The-Weekend carriage – which Nerlin himself had designed with the Magic Hat Winchflat had given him – Bacstairs, Nerlin's devoted manservant, guided the horses out of the castle and along the road towards the track leading into the mountains. They could have got up there in a few seconds using Winchflat's transporter – which they decided they would reserve for days of bad weather – but seeing as today was rather beautiful, damp and smelling nicely of fungus, travelling by horse added to the anticipation and general enjoyment.

Nerlin could not remember when he had last felt as happy as he did then. The sun was shining through a delicate cloud of pure white mist. The leaves looked greener than they had ever been before and the air was filled with skylarks singing their hearts out.[57]

Yes, they were only going away for the weekend, but it would be every weekend and surely it would only be a matter of time until one of his children decided they would like to be the ruler of this beautiful country.

Life was perfect.

'Who is Gertrude?' said a voice, breaking into his daydreams.

'What?'

'I said, who is Gertrude?' said Mordonna.

The entire world suddenly went dark, darker than the darkest thunderclouds. This didn't just happen inside Nerlin's head – it happened for real. Nerlin may not have been much use at magic, but hearing his sister's name, the name he had spent his entire adult life trying to forget, sent his brain into

---

[57] *This is just a weird expression that makes no sense at all, because at no point did any of the tiny songbirds' hearts actually leave their bodies. That only happened when they were fried for breakfast.*

hyper-space-overdrive-total-overload-freak-out-city.

Mordonna reeled back in horror. Then Nerlin fainted, and the darkness faded away as the world returned to normal.

'Pull over,' Mordonna shouted to Bacstairs.

They lifted the unconscious King of Transylvania Waters out of the carriage and laid him down on the grass beside the track.

'What was that about?' Mordonna exclaimed.

'Everything went black,' said Bacstairs, who hadn't been able to hear the 'G' word from where he had been sitting.

'Yes, I know that,' Mordonna replied. 'My husband did it. He has always been so useless at magic and yet he did the Total Darkness Spell, one of the most powerful spells in the universe. It's so powerful that most people don't even believe it exists. I certainly didn't, and yet I saw it with my own eyes.'

'I am speechless, my lady,' Bacstairs said, showing that he wasn't speechless at all.

'All I said was, "Who is Gertrude?"' Mordonna said.

'Gertrude, my lady?' said Bacstairs. 'That's just a funny old-lady name, isn't it? I've never met or even heard of anyone called Gertrude.'

'Indeed,' said Mordonna. 'But the name has an unbelievably powerful effect on your master. No matter what you do, you must never, ever say it in front of him.'

The name drifted through the air and into the ears of the still unconscious Nerlin, and the Total Darkness Spell returned, except the total darkness was not as totally dark as it had been when Nerlin had been conscious. It was more a sort of Quite Dark Shade of Grey Spell, which no one had ever done before and was rather attractive, though it could have been just a touch brighter.

Eventually the darkness faded and the late afternoon colour returned, which was exactly the same as the Quite Dark Shade of Grey Spell, but with a bit of colour and yellow stars in the sky. Nerlin slowly regained consciousness and for a while was unable to remember who or where he was.

Mordonna was very careful not to mention the 'G' name, but was desperate to find out exactly who this woman was and why she had such an unimaginable effect on Nerlin.

Had he fallen in love with someone else? Did he have a secret girlfriend? Nerlin had never once given the slightest sign of it and he didn't seem like the type to ever think of something like that, but then maybe Mordonna hadn't been giving him as much attention as she used to. She hadn't noticed any signs of restlessness or unhappiness, apart from the wanting-to-retire thing, and she thought they had sorted that out, at least for now. Or maybe a witch had cast a spell over him to lure him away from her. It wouldn't be the first time.[58]

But, try as she might, Mordonna couldn't think of any other reason for one woman's name to affect Nerlin so dramatically.

'What happened?' said Nerlin, as his head

---

[58] *See* The Floods 12: Bewitched.

cleared and he sat up. 'Did I slip out of the coach?'

'Yes, my darling,' Mordonna lied. 'I think you must have fallen asleep with all the excitement of going to the cottage.'

'Gosh,' said Nerlin. 'I never knew you could fall asleep from being excited about something.'

'Oh yes,' said Mordonna. 'It happens a lot. Surely you're not telling me it's never happened to you before?'

'I don't think so. Not that I can remember.'

'That's probably one of its side effects,' Mordonna explained. 'So when you wake up, you automatically forget that you fell asleep. It's a sort of natural defence mechanism to protect you.'

'From what?'

'Umm . . .'

'Falling asleep again,' said Bacstairs.

'Indeed,' said Mordonna.

'Oh.'

One of the two royal horses pulling the carriage looked at its mate and whispered, 'If you believe that, you'll believe anything.'

The other horse nodded and whispered back, 'Yeah. It's a good job you don't have to pass an intelligence test to be King.'

Both horses laughed so hard that they had to stop for a second and pee.

It was going to be a good weekend.

11

It WAS going to be a good weekend.

'I just wish I could be a fly on the wall, listening in on Mother talking to Daddy about you,' Betty said the next afternoon when she went back to see Gertrude.

'Would a magpie do?' said Gertrude.

'Magpie?'

'Yes, I've got a friend who is a magpie,' said Gertrude. 'And as everyone knows, as well as stealing shiny things and eating roadkill, magpies love stirring things up a bit. I'm sure if I asked my friend, he could fly up to your parents' cottage and eavesdrop.

'Also,' Gertrude continued, 'did you notice how

the world went dark for a minute or so yesterday afternoon?'

'I did,' said Betty. 'It was very weird. I thought it might have been you practising your magic.'

'No, it wasn't me,' said Gertrude. 'I reckon your father did something when your mother said my name.'

'No way,' said Betty. 'My father is really bad at magic.'

'I know, but I still think he did it,' said Gertrude. 'It just goes to show what a dramatic effect my name had on him. He also has nightmares where he dreams I am dead.'

'How do you know that?' said Betty.

'I have my contacts,' said Gertrude mysteriously.

She told Betty that she had been following the family ever since Nerlin had first met Mordonna and they ran away together. Gertrude knew about the Flood children and said that out of all of them she felt the closest affinity with Betty.

Betty was too polite and nervous to ask her aunt how she'd followed their lives for all these

years and Gertrude gave no hint of how she'd done it.[59]

'We have a lot in common,' Gertrude said, 'and when the time is right, I will pass the power of the Ultimate Super-Wizards on to you. For as it was given to me, I can only give it to one other person, and if I should die before I transfer this power then it will die with me.'

'Wow,' said Betty. 'I've got some quite good magical powers already, but I'm sure they're nothing like yours.'

'Indeed,' said Gertrude. 'What you have now are Standard Wizard powers, grade two or three, I would guess. Your powers are like a skateboard with three wheels missing compared to the Ultimate Super-Wizard, which is like a Bugatti Super Veyron car.'

Gertrude told Betty that the way the power transfer worked was all or nothing. She couldn't

---

[59] *Nor am I at liberty to tell you. Let's just say there were a lot of tweeting slugs and homing gherkins involved and leave it at that.*

give her niece one or two superpowers – she'd have to do everything in one go because there could only ever be one single witch or wizard with the Ultimate Super-Wizard powers.

'So does that mean once you complete the transfer, you will have no powers at all?' Betty asked.

'Not quite,' said Gertrude. 'Mine will be downgraded to Standard Wizard powers, grade one. You know, the basic things we all did when we were very young, like changing evil parsnips into lovely bars of chocolate.'

'Did you do that, Auntie?' said Betty, running over and throwing her arms round the old lady. 'I did that. I drove my mum crazy.'

'Me too. Still do,' said Gertrude.

Tears of happiness came into Gertrude's eyes. No one had ever cuddled her before. The years alone in the drains had been long and lonely, and Gertrude found herself wishing she had come up to the surface much earlier.

'You do realise, don't you,' she said, 'that once you have these powers you will be the most powerful

witch, not just on planet Earth, but in the entire universe, and there will be no witch or wizard whose powers will come anywhere near yours.'

'Wow,' said Betty, and then she realised what that meant.

Betty would be the ruler of Transylvania Waters, which would become the magic centre of the entire galaxy. She would even have enough power to create new galaxies if she wanted to. And because Gertrude with her awesome powers had stayed hidden away in the drains for so long, most wizards thought that whoever was in possession of the Ultimate Super-Wizard powers had died and they had been lost forever.

The old lady and the child stood in silence for a while as the colossal importance of all this sunk in.

'Right,' said Betty at last. 'I don't have to tell my parents any of this yet, do I?'

She explained to Gertrude that Nerlin wanted to retire and he had tried to get one of his children to take over as ruler, a role no one had wanted, and that Mordonna had made them agree to take over each weekend in the hope that one of them would want to take on the job full time.

'So I think it would be fun to make them all sweat for a while,' said Betty.

'You'd think anyone would jump at the chance of being a king or queen,' said Gertrude. 'Especially in a place as brilliant as Transylvania Waters.'

'Not really,' said Betty. 'I mean, the good bits like travelling around wearing a crown and going to other countries for state visits and getting your picture on postage stamps and that sort of stuff is only a tiny part of it. Most of it's pretty boring, like having to sit in judgement over two idiots arguing about who gets to kiss the enchanted frog and then deciding who has to pay for the mouthwash when the frog turns out to be a real frog and not a princess.'

'But when you are Queen, you won't have to bother with all that rubbish,' said Gertrude. 'You'll have the Ultimate Super-Wizard powers, so you can get other people to do the boring stuff while you enjoy life.'

'Yes, I suppose so,' said Betty.

'Just think of the fun you can have travelling the world with princes falling at your feet wanting to marry you,' said Gertrude.

'Did you do that?'

'No, I was stuck down the drains. Not a lot of princes live in drains and the ones who do are really weird. They like collecting strange things like purple growths on embarrassing parts of their bodies, and that's just the younger, more handsome ones. You wouldn't believe the state of the old princes with bits of themselves that keep falling off and have to be carried round in shopping bags,' said Gertrude. 'No, I decided a life alone was better than having a husband who shed skin every night.'

'There's still time, Auntie,' said Betty. 'Maybe you should come to Dreary. We can find you a nice, kind, oldish wizard who likes washing up and gardening. After all, once you move into your retirement cottage up in the mountains, you'll need someone to weed the deadly nightshade and prune the hemlock.'

'You're right,' said Gertrude. 'Once I downgrade

to Standard Wizard powers, grade one, I might not be able to do all that washing up and gardening using spells. We'll see, there's no rush.'

Betty realised that, even with her ultimate powers, her old aunt was anxious about returning to a world full of people. Although Gertrude had often been lonely, she had also liked being alone with none of modern life's complications, and the thought of sharing her life with a partner was pretty scary.

As the sun slipped down the back of the mountains and the moon woke up to take its place, Nerlin and Mordonna arrived at their cottage in the Enchanted Valley. Nerlin was pretty much back to normal, having no recollection of the 'G' word.

Mordonna was torn in several directions. The 'G' word wouldn't leave her alone. Should she ask Nerlin about it again or not? Maybe not, after what had happened the first time, but it was driving her crazy. Who was this Gertrude?

She decided to keep it to herself and wait until they got home, where she could confront Betty and demand an explanation.

It did take the edge off her weekend, though.

Nerlin, however, couldn't remember when he had felt happier. The cottage was even better than how he'd dreamt it to be. The weather was perfect – a lovely mist in the morning that slowly faded away as the new day's sunshine rose over the mountains. Everything tasted better than in his best memories and the silence in the valley was interrupted only by the birds singing in the trees. Not that Transylvania Waters or even Dreary were particularly noisy places. Everything was fitted with a silencer invented by Winchflat, so that the smallest and quietest things such as slugs,[60] as well as boiling kettles, did their business in silence.

The Enchanted Valley was not called the Enchanted Valley for nothing.[61]

---

[60] *One of Transylvania Waters's most popular music albums was* The Songs of the Slug. *Even if you turned the volume right up, all you could hear was a gentle squelchy noise as the slugs slipped towards a big cabbage and a faint rasping as they ate the cabbage leaves.*

[61] *And where I live –* The Promised Land *– is not called that without good reason.*

169

'It's going to be really hard going back to Dreary,' said Nerlin, and for once Mordonna found herself beginning to agree with him.

Mordonna liked being Queen. She enjoyed being in charge of everything, because although everyone adored King Nerlin, they all knew he was pretty useless as a wizard and that it was Mordonna who made the important decisions. But it seemed to suit everybody. Everyone looked forward to Monday mornings when a notice declaring Nerlin's orders for the following week was pinned up outside Castle Twilight.

The most anticipated and important notice was which biscuit was officially declared Biscuit of the Week. It was usually Custard Creams, though sometimes it was Bourbons.[62] Now and then, if Mordonna told Nerlin he needed to lose a little weight, everyone would spend the week eating Rich Tea biscuits, which are the sort of biscuits you eat when you know you shouldn't be eating between

---

[62] *My favourite.*

meals. The trouble with Rich Teas was that most people followed them with a bar of chocolate to make them more exciting. When Nerlin was feeling really happy, he advised all his subjects to have a big spoonful of condensed milk.[63]

Meanwhile, back in her room at Castle Twilight, Betty was thinking about deep and meaningful things.

When you are young, she thought, your parents are in charge. And when they were young, their parents were in charge of them. The thing is, people don't always wait until their parents die to take charge of things.

'So, my question is,' she said to Ffiona, 'how old do you have to be in order to be in charge? To put it another way, how old do your parents have to be for you to take over?'

'I reckon that would depend on your parents,' Ffiona said. 'I can't see your mother ever letting you take over.'

---

[63] *My extra, extra super favourite – even better than bacon.*

171

'Yes, you're probably right,' said Betty. 'Though Dad is really keen to retire and Mum is getting older.'

'Yes, but if none of you agree to take over as ruler, I reckon your mother will do it,' said Ffiona.

'Until we met Auntie Gertrude I would have agreed with you,' Betty replied. 'Though now that Mum thinks Auntie Gertrude might claim the throne, everything is different.'

'But your auntie doesn't want to be Queen.'

'Yes, but Mum and Dad don't know that,' said Betty. 'So I reckon I could persuade them to retire and let me take over.'

'I think you could have a fight on your hands,' said Ffiona. 'You know your mum doesn't like you doing anything better than she can.'

'Oh, I don't know,' Betty said and grinned. 'When Mum discovers that Gertrude has given me the Ultimate Super-Wizard powers and that Gertrude is the rightful ruler of Transylvania Waters and that she and Dad might get thrown into the dungeons, Mum might be persuaded to change her mind.'

The only problem Betty had was that she was

planning to give her parents' retirement cottage to Gertrude, but she soon discovered the matter could be easily fixed. Betty could just get Winchflat to clone the entire Enchanted Valley at the other end of the country, so then Gertrude would get the identical cottage and her parents could keep the original one. It would be a lot bigger than anything Winchflat had ever copied before, but Betty guessed that this was the sort of challenge her brother enjoyed.

In the meantime, Betty would carry on pretending that she did not want to take over as monarch.

'Why?' Ffiona asked.

'Just to be cantankerous,' said Betty. 'You know, for a laugh. I'm not going to do anything until all my brothers and sisters have had at least one turn each running the country. I also think that with each weekend up in the Enchanted Valley, Dad will love it more and more.'

'You're mean and wicked, you are,' said Ffiona with a smile.

'Yeah, great, isn't it?' said Betty.

'So, what nasty little law did you make this weekend, madam?' Mordonna asked when she and Nerlin returned to Castle Twilight.

'Law? Oh, I didn't bother,' said Betty, wearing her super-special-innocent expression on her face.

Mordonna was instantly suspicious and spent hours checking and searching until she finally had to admit that there didn't seem to have been any new laws registered since the last one she herself had created seven weeks ago making it illegal to eat custard in the bath.

Betty is up to something, she thought. And then she remembered . . .

. . . Gertrude.

Mordonna sent a servant to find her daughter immediately.

'Right, young lady, tell me right now – who is Gertrude?' she demanded.

'Didn't Daddy tell you?' said Betty, super-special-innocent expression still on her face.

'And you can wipe that super-special-innocent expression off your face right away!' Mordonna snapped.

'Did you forget to ask him?' said Betty. 'I told you to, remember?'

Mordonna told Betty what had happened when she'd asked Nerlin and how his reaction had been so dramatic that she'd been too scared to ask him again.

'The whole world went black,' she said. 'The Total Darkness Spell. You've most likely never heard of it or, if you have, you probably didn't think it was real like I did.'

Betty shook her head in wide-eyed innocence. Everything was going so well. It was hard not to burst out laughing.

'I noticed that,' she said. 'I thought some alien had come and stolen the sun. So he didn't tell you who Gertrude is, then?'

For the first time in her life, Betty thought her

mother was going to cry and she almost felt sorry for her.

'It must be another woman,' Mordonna said, as seven tears ran down her face onto her dress, where they burnt seven small holes before evaporating.

It hadn't occurred to Betty that this would happen.

'No, Mother, it isn't another woman,' she said. 'Well, actually, it is, but not in the way that you think. Father hasn't got a girlfriend or anything gross like that.'

'So, who is she then?' said Mordonna, pulling herself together.[64]

'Dad's sister.'

'Sister?' said Mordonna. 'He hasn't got a sister. He would have told me, otherwise.'

'Dad's twin sister.'

'I don't believe you,' said Mordonna. 'You've just made all this up to annoy me.'

'Then why did he do the Total Darkness Spell?'

---

[64] *Mordonna wasn't actually falling to bits. It's just an expression and another example of how silly our language often is.*

said Betty. 'And by the way, I do know about the spell.'

She then told her mother that not only was Gertrude really Nerlin's twin, but she was seven hours, seven minutes and seven seconds older than Nerlin and was therefore the rightful ruler of Transylvania Waters. If Mordonna had not already been whiter than fresh snow, she would have gone white. As it was, she could feel her blood turning white.

Mordonna's first thought was to accuse Betty of lying. It was exactly the sort of game her daughter would play. But then there was the Total Darkness Spell, and there was no way Nerlin would have had that sort of reaction to a wind-up.

Her second thought was to assume Gertrude was as useless at magic as her twin brother, so it would be pretty easy to get rid of her.

'I expect you're thinking Auntie Gertrude will be easy to get rid of, aren't you?' said Betty.

'No, of course not,' Mordonna lied.

'Good,' said Betty. 'Because she's got the Ultimate Super-Wizard powers and she could eat

you for breakfast, lunch and dinner.'

'Don't be silly,' said Mordonna. 'No one has the Ultimate Super-Wizard powers. The last wizard to have had them died before he could pass them on.'

Betty assured her mother that the powers had, in fact, been given to Gertrude. She nearly said that Gertrude was going to pass them on to her, but decided to keep that wonderful bit of information to herself – for the moment.

'So, where is this Gertrude?' said Mordonna. 'I think I should meet her. I'm sure we can sort something out.'

Yeah, right, Betty thought. *My mother the negotiator. NOT!*

'Auntie Gertrude will meet you when she is ready,' said Betty. 'She told me to let you know that, in the meantime, anything you want to say to her you can tell me and I'll pass it on.'

'Right. OK. Where is she, then?'

'Not here,' said Betty.

She's probably hiding back down the drains, Mordonna thought. *Daddy should have totally destroyed them when he had the chance. I think I should finish the job for him.*

Of course Gertrude was not down in the drains, but she and her niece both guessed that Mordonna would assume she was and would set about destroying Gertrude's home. And because there were bits of Mordonna's brain that were just like her crazy father Ex-King Quatorze's, she could sometimes do ridiculous rage-inspired things without thinking about the consequences.

'By the way, Mother, it wouldn't be a good idea to blow up the drains like your mad dad tried to do. First off, Auntie G isn't actually down there, and if you did that, it would block up every lavatory in town,' said Betty.

She then told her mother that she would leave her to think things over and to maybe try to approach Nerlin about the whole thing.

'You don't have to worry about Dad doing the Total Darkness Spell again. Auntie has put a temporary block on it,' said Betty.

'Oh, and one more thing,' she continued.

179

'Best not have me followed when I go to see Auntie G again. The Ultimate Super-Wizard powers are unimaginably awesome, and if you send someone after me not only will they be turned into burnt toast, you yourself will be turned into the scorched jam on top of the toast.'

Mordonna said nothing, but she refused to believe that any sister of Nerlin's could be smart enough to outwit her, and as far she she was concerned the Ultimate Super-Wizard powers were made up to scare people.

'No offence, Mother. That's just what Auntie Gertrude told me,' Betty added.

13

The worst thing for Mordonna was that there was no one she could talk to about it. Normally, she'd go to Nerlin whenever there was a problem. It wasn't that he often had anything useful to offer, but he always had a sympathetic ear. So Mordonna decided to talk to Ffiona's mother, Edna Hulbert, who was the closest thing she had to a close friend, which was not close at all.

Edna Hulbert, like the rest of her family, was not a witch or a wizard. She was a human.

But, as humans go, she's pretty good, Mordonna said to herself. *It's just that talking to her about wizard stuff is like talking to someone in a foreign language. There'll be so much she won't understand.*

'You mean, your husband isn't the King of Transylvania Waters after all?' said Edna, when Mordonna explained that it was the oldest child who became the monarch, regardless of whether they were male or female. 'I didn't even know he had a sister.'

'You, me and everyone,' said Mordonna. 'I can't believe he never told me.'

'Husbands can be quite devious sometimes,' said Edna. 'Mine never told me he liked LEGO until I found boxes and boxes of it hidden in his shed. I used to wonder what he was doing in there for hours on end. It never occurred to me he was playing with little pieces of plastic.'[65]

'Yes, but having a secret sister is a bit different to having some secret toys,' said Mordonna.

'Maybe his sister doesn't want the job,' Edna suggested.

'Betty says she does,' Mordonna replied. 'I mean, who wouldn't want to be the ruler of the greatest country on Earth?'

---

[65] *There are some brilliant and talented people who have quite a lot of LEGO.*

'Yes, well, I don't want to sound rude, but we both know our daughters are not completely, um, err, sort of addicted to always telling the truth,' said Edna.

'That's true,' said Mordonna, seeing a straw she might be able to clutch.

But the situation was one of those you could only really see the worse side of. Mordonna wanted to believe that Gertrude had no desire to be Queen, but if that was the case, why had she come up the drains and sought out Betty to tell her who she was, if not to make trouble and claim the throne?

'I don't know what to do,' Mordonna said. 'I told Betty I wanted to speak to her aunt so we could maybe sort things out, but Betty said Gertrude doesn't want to see me.'

'Hmm . . . could you have her followed next time Betty goes to see her?'

'Yes, except Betty said she advised me not to do that.'

'And you let her tell you what to do?' said Edna. 'Surely not!'

'You're absolutely right, but Betty says that Gertrude's got the Ultimate Super-Wizard powers,' said Mordonna, then explained how this meant Gertrude was more powerful than all the other witches and wizards on Earth and could pretty well do anything she wanted.

'She could be bluffing.'

'That's true, and five years ago I would have taken her on,' said Mordonna sadly. 'But you know, we're all getting older and I'm beginning to think that my beloved husband has got the right idea when he says he wants to retire to our cottage in the Enchanted Valley and let someone younger take over.'

Edna agreed. She and Mr Hulbert had been talking about going to live in a bungalow by the sea, except it would mean leaving Transylvania Waters, which they had grown to love. Of course, they could always retire to a bungalow by the lake, but a lake is not the seaside and for as long as the Hulberts could remember they had agreed that one day they would go and live by the sea and wake up each morning to the sound of waves crashing on a beach of golden sand with seagulls calling through the spray.

'Winchflat could make you a Wave and Seagull Machine and you could move to the far end of the lake,' said Mordonna. 'Except bungalows are illegal in Transylvania Waters because they are very boring.'

'Oh,' said Edna, who had always dreamt of retiring to a bungalow with a few garden gnomes, a little fountain and some honeysuckle.

It was hard to imagine Mordonna as someone who might retire. Queens don't do that sort of thing. They go on and on past their use-by dates until their own children are too old to take over. This didn't happen in the good old days. Back then, when the children thought it was time for their turn to be King or Queen, they simply got rid of their parents. Unfortunately, this fine old tradition has died out almost everywhere.

And it didn't look as if any of the Flood children were thinking about bumping their parents off. None of them wanted to take over. They all thought it was a boring dead-end job.

At least, this was what Mordonna and Nerlin were led to believe. Neither of them had the faintest clue that Betty had other ideas. Nerlin would have been delighted to know that his beloved youngest child actually wanted to be Queen. On the other hand, Mordonna would have been furious. It would mean that Betty would've won the battle she had started with her mother when she and Ffiona had opened their own restaurant a couple of years earlier.[66 & 67]

Mordonna suspected that Betty was up to something, but she had no idea what it was. It was very strange that her daughter had not made a new law during her first weekend as ruler. For now, though, Mordonna decided to let it go. She told

---

[66] *See* The Floods 11: Disasterchef.

[67] *Betty and Ffiona's restaurant, The Devil's Kitchen, had been a huge success and there were now sixteen of them dotted around Transylvania Waters, with branches planned for Patagonia and Tristan da Cunha. Neither Betty nor Ffiona were involved in the day-to-day running of the restaurants, due to the employment of highly trained zombies who guaranteed that none of their bits would fall into the food.*

herself she would just keep an eye on things and be ready for whatever Betty tried to do. But in the back of Mordonna's mind grew the thought that she was getting older and the day would finally come when one of her children would take over.

She just hoped it wouldn't be Betty.

14

The next Friday afternoon, while Betty made herself scarce, Mordonna collected her other children together and spun round with her eyes closed.

This time she chose the twins, Morbid and Silent, to rule the kingdom for the weekend.

Obviously Mordonna could only pick one of them, but little did she know that earlier in the day Morbid and Silent had agreed that neither of them would admit who was who if they were chosen.

'Right, Morbid, you are King this weekend,' said Mordonna.

'No, he's Morbid,' said Morbid, pointing at Silent.

'Oh, yes,' said Mordonna, who had never been able to tell them apart but would never admit to it. 'So, Silent, you will be King for the weekend.'

'But I'm Morbid,' said Silent.

This went on backwards and forwards for five minutes until Mordonna spat out a string of swear words and a fireball, and told the twins that they were both King.

'Can't do that,' said Valla. 'That's democracy, which everyone knows is illegal in all witch and wizard countries.'

'Exactly,' said Winchflat. 'I mean, who knows what could happen? Ordinary people would want to vote and stuff like that. It would be chaotic, and to keep the peace the twins would have to turn them all into tadpoles.'

'Or boiled eggs,' said Morbid.

'Hard-boiled eggs,' said Silent.

Mordonna began banging her head against the wall and swearing a lot more. Maybe this weekend cottage part-time King or Queen thing wasn't worth all the trouble. It had seemed like a pretty good idea at the time – every weekend up in the Enchanted Valley just lazing around. Now she wasn't so sure.

It's Betty, I know it is, she said to herself. *She's doing all this.*

Mordonna was right, though everyone denied it when she confronted them.

'Betty?' said Valla. 'You mean, our lovely little sister Betty?'

'Yes,' said Mordonna. 'She's trying to make trouble, isn't she?'

'What, our angelic little sister?' said Winchflat. 'Oh, Mother, why would she do that for?'

'Power,' snapped Mordonna.

'Power?' said Merlinmary. 'Sweet little Betty? What on earth made you think that?'

'She hates me, that's why,' said Mordonna.

'Don't be silly, Mother. Betty adores both you and Father,' said Satanella.

'Yes, she loves your father but it's clear she hates me,' said Mordonna. 'She's got you all taken in with her big blue eyes and golden curls and pretence that she can't really do magic.'

None of Betty's brothers or sisters would agree with their mother, even though secretly they all knew she was right.

Ever since Betty had been born, her siblings had known that one day she would outshine them all. Mordonna, on the other hand, had only realised this as Betty had grown up, knowing full well that there would be plenty of future showdowns with her youngest daughter.

Betty's brothers and sisters loved their youngest sister, not in spite of how she was and would be, but because of her ability to successfully lead the kingdom. They loved the idea of Betty becoming Queen, ruling not just Transylvania Waters, but anywhere and everywhere. It eliminated a lot of potential problems like one of the Floods siblings marrying someone who turned out to be dreadful and tried to ruin their monarch. They knew that if and when Betty got married it would be to someone who was not only brilliant but also completely under her power, much like her father was under

Mordonna's control.[68]

Of course, none of Betty's siblings knew about Gertrude and the Ultimate Super-Wizard powers. If they had, they would have felt safer talking to each other about it.

So that weekend, after Nerlin and Mordonna had gone up to the cottage, all the Flood children gathered together in a secret meeting room high up in one of Castle Twilight's towers.

Even Satanella was there, whose spell in The Naughty Tower had quietened her down a bit. She was still a selfish air-head, perfectly qualified for the popular TV show *The Why Factor*, but at least she'd stopped talking about herself all the time and

---

[68] *The Flood children already knew that Betty would one day become the ruler. So why, I hear you ask, were they all so adamant in their refusal to become King or Queen when Nerlin asked them to? Well, the reason for this was, although they all knew individually that Betty would end up in charge, they never spoke to each other about it and certainly not to Betty because there was always the worry that Mordonna would find out what they were thinking and try to do something to Betty to keep her from her destiny. And by the way, I didn't actually hear you ask this, I just hoped you were intelligent enough to think it.*

spending hours in front of the mirror.

There were no husbands, wives, children or friends in the tower – just the seven children. None of them knew who had called the meeting. There had been no conversations or messages, just a time and place that appeared in each of their heads, a time and place that had been put there by the eighth person in the room.

Gertrude.

'OK, everyone,' Betty said, when they were all sitting in a circle around the edge of the small room, 'I would like you to meet our aunt.'

'Aunt?' said at least three of them.

'What aunt?' said the others.

'Auntie Gertrude,' said Betty. 'She's our father's twin sister.'

'But Father hasn't got any sisters or brothers,' said Winchflat. 'Otherwise he would've told us, or we would've met them.'

'He kept it a secret,' Betty explained. 'Even our mother didn't know.'

'Why?' said the twins, who were especially

delighted to discover their father was a twin too.

'Oh no. I know what you're going to say,' said Valla. 'Father is younger than his sister, isn't he?'

'Clever boy,' said Gertrude.

'So you are the ruler of Transylvania Waters, not Father,' said Winchflat.

'Technically,' Gertrude replied. 'Except it's the last thing I want to be. I suspect that none of you want the job, either?'

Everyone agreed, apart from Betty.

'Except me,' she said.

The others all let out a great sigh. They felt as if they had been holding their breaths forever. Then they all began talking at once, telling each other how they always sort of knew that Betty would one day be Queen.

'It's her destiny, isn't it?' said Satanella, thankful that she wouldn't be made to do the job because, as everyone knew, being a Queen was really bad for your complexion.

'Indeed,' said Gertrude, 'from before she was born.'

'Wow,' said the twins.

Gertrude explained that although she had spent all her life, until a few weeks ago, down in the drains, she had always kept an eye on her brother and his life, wife and children. She believed that all of Nerlin's children were brilliant, each in their own special way, but it was Betty and her unique combination of personality traits that made her the most suitable one to rule Transylvania Waters.

'This isn't meant to make the rest of you feel inferior to Betty,' she said. 'It's just that I think she's the best equipped to handle any possible threat that may come in the future. Don't forget that even the greatest wizard of all time, your grandfather Merlin, was overthrown by the evil King Quatorze.'

Everyone agreed that Betty should be the next ruler. There was no jealousy at all. In fact, the Flood children felt rather relieved that they wouldn't have to take the job.

Then Betty explained that they shouldn't tell their parents about it. She said she wanted her parents to think that none of them aspired to take

over, and that Nerlin and Mordonna had to stay King and Queen until they died.[69]

'Except I told Mother about Auntie Gertrude last weekend,' Betty said. 'And that she had come from the drains to take over the throne and there was every possibility that Mother and Father would get thrown into gaol for Monarchy Theft, which is a really serious crime.'

'You are so mean,' said Merlinmary.

But everyone thought it was hilarious, including Merlinmary.

'All I really want is a lovely little cottage high up in the mountains,' said Gertrude. 'A place I can go to retire and spend the rest of my days growing chrysanthemums and puppies, and getting visits from you and your children and their children and their children.'

'That's the same thing Dad wants,' said Satanella. 'He's built a cottage just like . . . oh, mmm.'

'Exactly,' said Morbid. 'We can keep on

---

[69] *Which, as they were witch and wizard, could mean waiting around for hundreds of years.*

pretending that Auntie Gertrude wants to be Queen and maybe even put Mother and Father in gaol. Then, after a few months, they'll agree to give our aunt the cottage in exchange for her moving there and giving up any claims to the throne.'

'Couldn't we just build another cottage?' said Valla.

'Winchflat's already taken care of that,' said Betty. 'But let's keep that to ourselves for the moment.'

Everyone agreed to Betty's plan. It would break the monotony of having to be in charge each weekend and everyone would end up living happily ever after.

'Aren't you forgetting something?' asked Valla.

'What?'

'I can't see Mother going away quietly,' he said. 'Especially if she thinks Betty's going to be Queen.'

'I'm quite sure she'll be furious,' said Betty with a smile. 'But if Mother thinks the other only option is being thrown into gaol by Queen Gertrude, she won't really have any choice.'

'I suppose it'll just come down to who's got the most powerful magic,' said Valla.

'Not really,' said Gertrude.

'Are you sure?' said Winchflat. 'Mother can get pretty awesome when she's angry.'

'Oh yes, we're sure,' said Betty, and told them about the Ultimate Super-Wizard powers.

'Does Mother know this?' Winchflat asked.

'Oh, yes,' said Betty. 'Though I imagine she'll be telling herself that she has more power.

'And,' Betty added, 'she doesn't know that when I become Queen, Auntie Gertrude is going to transfer the powers to me.'

'Indeed,' said Gertrude, 'but we'll keep that little treat from your parents for now too.'

Since the time Betty had met Gertrude in the forest, the old witch had dusted most of the cobwebs out of her brain and been practising her spells. So she decided to give them all a little demonstration of a few of the safer and smaller things the Ultimate Super-Wizard powers could do. Gertrude reached out her hand into the empty air and grabbed at something invisible.

'Now,' she said, 'I want each of you to think of something that you would like to see appear as I throw my hand up and open it. Don't tell me what it is. I will tell you what you're thinking of.'

Gertrude held her arm out in front of her at face-level, and blew on her closed hand before raising it above her head and opening her fingers. As she did this, she turned to each of the seven Flood children one by one.

'First, the twins,' she said, and started laughing.

There was a flash of light and there in front of Gertrude were the twins. Except they were twin twins – two Morbids and two Silents.

'Well,' Morbid explained, 'we both think things are better in twos, so we were wondering if they would be even better two times two.'

'Are they real?' said Betty. 'Not just brilliant holograms?'

'What do you think?' said Gertrude. 'Can you pick out the original Morbid and Silent?'

No one could.

'Wow,' said Betty, particularly impressed after remembering how flaky her aunt's magic had been when they'd first met.

Betty was the only one who knew about the invisible Undo Button on Gertrude's forehead,

which the old witch now touched to make the copy twins vanish. Before the actual twins could complain, Gertrude turned to Valla and raised her hand again.

The air in the room grew thick and heavy, and everyone moved as though they were in one of those nightmares where you wanted to run away but couldn't because your legs felt like they were stuck in thick treacle. Except the thick treacle was not treacle. It was blood.

This was Valla's favourite fantasy.

'OMG,' he said.

'Is it real blood?' said Betty.

Valla scooped some of the liquid in his hand and drank it.

'Oh yes, it's real blood, all right,' he said, drinking more. 'Human, too.'

'Human?' said Winchflat. 'Which human?'

'All of them,' said Gertrude.

'What?' said everyone.

'All of them,' said Gertrude. 'A human body has approximately five litres of blood, and there's quite a few hundred litres of blood here. So I just took one

pinprick of blood from every living human on Earth.'

'OMG,' said Valla again. 'You've made the ultimate cocktail.'

'Well, I think it's gross,' said Betty, 'but seriously impressive.'

'Indeed, little sister,' said Winchflat.

By then Valla had drunk all that he could and was filling up as many containers as he could get his hands on. Everyone else felt as if they were going to throw up,[70] but before they did Gertrude tapped her Undo Button and the blood vanished – including the stuff Valla had collected.[71]

Then it was Winchflat's turn.

The room grew and grew, not dark but enormous and bright with shelves and tables and cupboards everywhere. The place became so large, it was almost impossible to make out where the furthest wall was. And on every shelf there were

---

[70] *Please don't even try and imagine what throwing up into a sea of blood looks, feels and smells like. Just accept that it's one of the grossest things ever.*

[71] *Though he did get to keep the stuff he'd actually swallowed.*

electronics and gadgets and machines – every single one that had been known to exist. Some of them had been no more than fantasies, made-up things from science-fiction movies, but here they were and here they worked.

'I do not think I have died and gone to heaven,' said Winchflat. 'I am in heaven, and please, please, please, lovely dearest auntie, let me keep it all!'

'Later,' said Gertrude. 'Remember, this is just a demo.'

'But . . .' Winchflat began.

'Don't worry, dear boy,' said Gertrude. 'When the time comes for me to transfer the Ultimate Super-Wizard powers to your sister, she can bring all this back. And that goes for all of you.'

Not that she nor Betty needed to have worried, but this promise meant that Betty would have one hundred percent support from her siblings forever.

While this magic had been happening, Satanella had been looking at her reflection in the window. Since her mother had changed her from a small dog into a beautiful girl, Satanella had spent

so much time brushing her long dark hair that she now had to wear elastic bandages on both her wrists because of RVI.[72]

Having spent many happy years chasing sticks and red rubber balls, Satanella now spent most of her time chasing admirers, though deep in her heart – not that she would ever admit it – it did not have the same excitement she had felt sinking her teeth into a perfect red rubber ball, with or without added squeaky. She now looked down on her brothers and sisters where once they had played together. One night she woke up, and for a few seconds wished she was still a small dog. But she would never dare say this out loud.

'Me, me, me,' she said to Gertrude.

'Are you sure?' Gertrude replied.

'Of course I am,' Satanella snapped.

'OK,' Gertrude said, raising her hand.

All the walls turned into mirrors and in front of these were a thousand photographers pointing their

---

[72] *Repetitive Vanity Injury.*

cameras at Satanella. Fifty dopey princes and actors and actor-princes and prince-actors surrounded her with over sixty-four brain cells.[73] They 'oooed' and 'ahh-ed' and showered her with roses and diamonds, though some of the admirers had got their bunches of roses the wrong way round and were now impaled on the thorns.

'Out of the way, out of the way,' Satanella shouted at them. 'The photographers can't see me properly.'

She held up her hand to shoo them off, then screamed and burst into tears.

'I've broken a fingernail,' she cried.

Satanella's brothers and sisters felt even more sick than they had been when they were in Valla's pool of blood, and it was only Gertrude's quick action in pressing her Undo Button that stopped them from vomiting all over their self-important sister.

'Anyone would think you used to be a cat,' said Betty. 'Not a dog.'

---

[73] *Not each, obviously. The brain cells were shared amongst the admirers.*

'Now, before we do Merlinmary's wish, everyone should put on a thick pair of rubber wellies and gloves,' said Gertrude.

Suddenly, the air came alive. It sparkled and crackled and everyone's hair stood on end. Outside, far away in space, the sun grew a fraction dimmer as some of its energy was channelled into Merlinmary. Bolts of lightning danced around the room, narrowly missing everyone apart from Satanella's hair, which it frazzled into burnt charcoal. Satanella burst into tears again and ran from the tower.

'I hope she doesn't go too far,' said Gertrude.

She was about to explain that her Undo Button had a limited range, but stopped herself. It seemed a good idea to keep the knowledge of the Undo Button from the children apart from Betty.

Besides, Satanella needs to be brought down a peg or two, Gertrude thought to herself.

She pressed her forehead. The lightning disappeared and the sun grew brighter again. Because Satanella was partly out of range of the Undo Button's power, the hair on the left side of

her head returned to normal, but on the right it was frizzy and burnt.[74] Satanella vowed she would stay in her room until it grew back nicely again.

No one missed her.

Finally, Gertrude turned to Betty and raised her hand.

'Well, now,' she said, 'I know what you want, and I could actually produce a copy of him, but I'm not going to. You are dreaming of a wonderful, mysterious wizard who will come to Transylvania Waters and sweep you off your feet.'

Betty blushed and nodded. By now everyone had realised that Betty's true love and future husband was NOT going to be Prince Bert. They grinned and agreed it was better kept as a surprise.

But deep down, both Gertrude and Betty knew that this really wasn't what the young witch wanted. The main reason Gertrude could tell exactly what Betty desired was because she knew that Betty was the one true witch to rule all others. Even though

---

[74] *And what do we learn from this? If you are having a bad hair day, do not leave the room and keep very, very still.*

Betty looked the most human-like, Gertrude could see herself in her brother's youngest child. So, ever since they'd met face to face a few days before, Gertrude had been subtly re-programming Betty's brain so that now the young witch was really keen to become Queen. Not that Betty had needed much mind-bending in the first place.

15

Meanwhile, up in the Enchanted Valley, Mordonna and Nerlin were relaxing at their beautiful cottage. Well, Nerlin was, but Mordonna couldn't. No amount of chamomile tea or deadly nightshade and stinging nettle herbal baths could make her forget Betty's news.

There's nothing for it, Mordonna thought. *I'm going to have to talk to him.*

She decided to take some precautions to lessen the chance of Nerlin freaking out again. First of all, she would wait until it was night time to ask him, so that if he did do the Total Darkness Spell, no one would be able to tell.

Actually half the world would know, but they'll

*all be a long way away on the other side of the globe,
so who cares?* Mordonna said to herself.

Mordonna would get Nerlin as relaxed
as possible with a huge mug of mandrake and
chamomile tea, followed by a bowl of his favourite
festerweed and scrubble ice-cream, which always put
him in a dreamy mood. But what Mordonna hadn't
realised was that for all his freaking out and fainting,
Nerlin had been completely aware Mordonna had
spoken his sister's name. He knew it would only be
a matter of time before she would bring it up again.

So when Nerlin was full of ice-cream and
mandrake and tucked up in bed in his favourite
rat-skin pyjamas, Mordonna said as gently as she
could:

'So, my darling, I, umm, er . . .'

'Want to know who Gertrude is, I expect?'
said Nerlin.

'Oh, umm, yes.'

'She's my sister,' said Nerlin.

He then spent several hours explaining why
he had never told Mordonna about Gertrude and

that included the fact that his sister was older than him and should really, under wizard law, be the ruler of Transylvania Waters, but she had stayed behind when Nerlin had escaped, and then later on when Nerlin and Mordonna had come back with their children and rescued the rest of his family from the drains and overthrown Mordonna's evil father, who had taken control of Transylvania Waters, Gertrude had still not appeared so Nerlin had told himself that she must be dead, otherwise why would she not want to come up into the beautiful paradise that was Transylvania Waters?

Some of the sentences that Nerlin spoke were so long that he fainted from lack of oxygen five or six times.[75]

'So I sort of hoped she was dead, but I knew in my heart that she wasn't,' he continued. 'I told myself that if she had chosen to live in the drains for so long she must have gone completely Doolally and probably thought she was a teapot and would

---

[75] *Do NOT try this at home or anywhere that isn't home.*

212

be declared insane, which would disqualify her from being Queen, unlike in human royal families where being Doolally is considered one of the qualifications.'

'Well, I'm afraid to tell you that she is neither dead nor Doolally,' said Mordonna. 'And she is no longer living in the drains.'

'I suppose now she wants to claim her rightful inheritance,' said Nerlin. 'Not that I would really mind. I mean, it's not like any of our children want the job.'

'Yes, I know, but technically we have stolen the throne from her,' said Mordonna. 'We have committed treason and could be thrown in gaol or even have our heads chopped off, like what happened to your cousin Perlin in Barvarania.'

'It didn't do him much harm though, did it?' said Nerlin. 'Apart from the headaches.'

'I can't spend the rest of my life in gaol,' said Mordonna. 'I'm too beautiful to get slowly eaten away by mould.'

'So what are we going to do?'

'I think we have to kill your sister,' said Mordonna.

'You can't,' Nerlin replied. 'She's got the Ultimate Super-Wizard powers.'

'So your beloved daughter Betty has mentioned,' said Mordonna. 'I don't believe in those powers. I think the story's just made up to frighten people.'

'No, it's real,' said Nerlin.

'How come your sister got the Ultimate Super-Wizard powers and not you?' Mordonna asked.

'Our Great, Great, Great plus twenty-seven more Greats Grandfather Flood liked her more than me,' Nerlin explained. 'She used to take him hemlock cordial when he became old and bed-ridden.'

'Hold on, hold on,' said Mordonna. 'If he had the Ultimate Super-Wizard powers, why couldn't he just cast a spell on himself and become young and healthy again?'

'You really don't know anything about the Ultimate Super-Wizard powers, do you?'

'You mean, apart from the fact that there's no

such thing?' said Mordonna.

'The holder of the Ultimate Super-Wizard powers cannot perform spells on themselves,' Nerlin explained. 'If they did the wrong thing and the spell turned out to be a disaster, they might not be able to reverse it, and not only would that have seriously dangerous consequences, it could probably destroy the powers themselves forever.'[76]

'Yes, well, it all sounds like a load of fairy floss,' said Mordonna. 'I think we should kill your sister.'

'Perhaps it might be a better idea to go talk to her?' Nerlin suggested.

'I don't know where she is,' said Mordonna.

'Ask Betty.'

'She won't tell me,' said Mordonna. 'And Betty already warned me not to have her followed. Maybe she'll tell you. You could let her know that you would love to see your long-lost sister.'

'All right,' said Nerlin. 'I'll see what I can do.'

---

[76] *Of course, Nerlin didn't know about the Undo Button. This meant that what Nerlin had just told Mordonna was both completely wrong and completely rubbish.*

'And then we'll kill her,' said Mordonna.

Killing things – unless they were things you were going to eat, like snakes, slugs and things that didn't begin with 's' – was not something Nerlin thought Mordonna would do. As the world's top witch, Mordonna had never seemed to have any vicious killer characteristics, but perhaps the threat Gertrude presented was just too powerful for his wife to ignore.

'It's about survival,' she said.

'But she will kill you before you even get close to her,' said Nerlin. 'Or do something far worse if she feels like it.'

'You mean worse than being killed?' said Mordonna. 'What on earth could be worse than that?'

Nerlin thought for a bit. He made a few suggestions that Mordonna dismissed until he said: 'She could make you really ugly with warts, droopy bits and missing teeth, and she could make your eyes dull and beige-coloured, and then she could make you live for a very, very long time.'

'She couldn't do that,' Mordonna said, though there were doubts in her mind.

'She could and probably would,' said Nerlin. 'One of the extra abilities the holder of the Ultimate Super-Wizard powers has, is knowing someone's deepest fears and using that against them.'

'I still think you should try to see your sister,' said Mordonna.

'Yes, but there will be no making-her-dead attempts, or thoughts like that,' Nerlin replied.

'OK, if you say so.'

Of course, Nerlin had known his wife long enough to be able to tell in an instant when she was lying. This was one of those instances.

Oh well, he said to himself. *If she does try anything and Gertrude turns her into a really ugly old crone, at least I'll have the satisfaction of saying, 'I told you so'.*

I can't believe I just thought that, he added.

On Nerlin's face was a little smile, which he hid from his wife by coughing and putting his hand over his mouth.

16

'Your mother tells me that you have met my dear sister,' Nerlin said to Betty upon his return at Castle Twilight, after his partly relaxing, partly weird and partly freaky weekend at the cottage.

'Yes, Daddy, she's lovely,' Betty replied.

Father and daughter were sitting alone in one of the tower rooms, looking out the window. The last beams of the afternoon sun glowed like fire over the roofs of the town, and in the distance the golden light swayed across the water of Lake Tarnish. The sun eventually slipped down behind the mountains at the far end of Transylvania Waters and the air began to grow cold. As if controlled by the setting sun, which of course, being in a land of magic, it was, the wood waiting in the fireplace came alight in the room and began to warm the evening air.

'I would love to see Gertrude again,' said Nerlin, which, in some ways, was true. She was his sister, after all, and it had been such a long time and so much had happened since the siblings had last been together.

'There were times,' Nerlin continued, 'when I wondered if she was even still alive.'

Nerlin sounded as if he really wanted nothing more than to be reunited with his long-lost sister and Betty appeared to believe him one hundred percent.[77]

'I'm sure we can arrange something,' said Betty, with the sweet, innocent facial expression she was so good at.

The sweet, innocent act totally took Nerlin in. It always had, despite Mordonna telling him over and over again that it was all just put on. But Nerlin was one of those people who always saw the very best in

---

[77] *Of course she didn't. She believed him about thirty-seven percent.*

people, even when it wasn't there.[78] He could never accept that his youngest child could even think of doing anything devious, never mind actually doing it. If someone fell over on a banana skin that Betty had deliberately dropped in front of them, Nerlin would say how sad it was for poor Betty that the banana

---

[78] *TOP TIP: This is NOT a good idea, no matter what people tell you.*

had slipped out of her dainty little hands just at that moment. It drove Mordonna mad, but nothing she said could ever change her husband's mind.

Betty had known this her entire life and had used it many times in all sorts of little ways to get things from her father and to wind up her mother.

'I'll get in touch with Auntie Gertrude tomorrow and see what we can sort out,' said Betty.

'Maybe I could come with you?'

'No, I think it would be better if I saw her alone first,' Betty replied.

'I wonder if she got married,' Nerlin mused. 'Maybe she's got children. You could have cousins.'

And if Gertrude does have children and ends up claiming the throne, it will be her children who will continue to rule our wonderful kingdom, Nerlin thought.

Betty knew that Gertrude had never been married or had any children, but she said nothing. She thought that there was no point making things any easier for her parents, for the moment.

This was enough to put Mordonna's original

thought of murdering Gertrude into the bit of his head that was used for storing ideas that might actually be used. Unlike his wife and most of his children, this was not a very big part of his brain and because it had been so long since Nerlin had used it, there were cobwebs inside.

So now he felt guilty, really guilty for allowing this thought in. If Gertrude wanted to take over the throne, who was he to stand in her way? Mordonna's husband, that's who he was. He could hear her voice echoing round and round his brain and saying:

Kill her, kill her, kill her.

Nerlin was getting more and more stressed and confused. He wanted to pour his heart out to Betty, but the thought of what Mordonna would do to him if he did stopped him from telling his daughter.

It was a long, lonely night. Nerlin couldn't sleep, so he went down to the kitchen for a mug of hot Silo,[79] but that didn't work and he was still

---

[79] *Which is the wizard's answer to Milo, where the malt and the milk are replaced with groutweed and ditch water.*

awake. Bacstairs followed him round and round until Nerlin handed him three mugs of cold Silo, which, as a dutiful servant, he drank himself, only to fall fast asleep in the dog's basket on top of the dog, who had always adored Bacstairs and was happier than he had ever been in his whole life, even happier than the time his greatest enemy, Grummo the kitchen cat,[80] had fallen into the toaster and got all his fur burnt off down one side.[81]

Nerlin returned to bed, and as the sun came up he finally fell asleep and missed breakfast. As he snored away, Betty went out into the forest to see Gertrude.

Of course, Gertrude already knew everything that was going on. When you have the Ultimate Super-Wizard powers, you have spies absolutely everywhere, even inside your enemies' heads. You have the normal spies, like magpies and cockroaches,

---

[80] *There were actually dozens of cats in the kitchen, but Grummo was unique in that he was not a recipe ingredient.*

[81] *The toaster had been on the bagel setting, which only heats up on one side.*

but you also have invisible spies that you just imagine. All you have to do is think of where you would like to be spying and an invisible fly on the wall appears or, rather, doesn't appear. None of the normal spy-detectors can pick them up and neither can any of the abnormal ones. So Gertrude had heard every word that had passed between Mordonna and Nerlin up at the cottage and all the stuff between Nerlin and Betty back at Castle Twilight. She had also read the secret thoughts inside everyone's heads.

'So, what would you like to do?' Gertrude asked Betty. 'And I must say, I'm quite enjoying this.'

'I knew you would,' Betty replied, grinning.

'Yes, I thought winding your mother up and making your poor parents think I wanted the throne seemed a bit childish at first – and I apologise for that, my dear,' said Gertrude. 'It's just that stuck down in the drains I never had time for a childhood. I just went straight from being a toddler to being old. I missed out on all the stuff in between, and it's only now I realise that's actually the best bit.'

'It is, it is,' said Betty and gave her aunt a big hug.

'Well, I can't say I'm enjoying a second childhood, because I never had a first one,' Gertrude said. 'But I'm jolly well going to make sure I get the best out of this one.

'I might even get a boyfriend,' she added. 'I've never had one of those.'

The two of them agreed that once Gertrude transferred the Ultimate Super-Wizard powers to Betty, her niece would give her a makeover.

'I wouldn't want to appear like some pathetic old lady done up to look young,' said Gertrude.

'You won't,' said Betty. 'You'll just have a lot less wrinkles and no grey hair, and above all else, you will look ten, no, let's say twenty years younger than my mother.'

'You are so wicked,' said Gertrude, giving Betty a hug. 'Do you think you could teach me how to be wicked?'

'Sure, no problem,' said Betty. 'But what are we going to do now?'

'Well, if I'm not mistaken,' said Gertrude, 'your parents have just set up a plan so that when you agree to bring your father to meet me, your mother will disguise herself as an old washerwoman – not very original, I might add – and she will follow you at a safe distance with the help of a tame homing pigeon. So this is what I suggest we do . . .'

The next day after breakfast Nerlin and Betty set out for the forest. Betty took a complicated route that would be impossible for Nerlin to remember, even if he were hypnotised. Betty had got Gertrude to tattoo the route on the back of her eyelids, so if she came to a turn on the path all she had to do was shut her eyes for a second to see which way to go.

Nerlin had even forgotten which turn went where before they left town, but he didn't care. After all, there were times when he got lost inside Castle Twilight, where there were so many corridors and rooms that looked the same.

Mordonna, now heavily disguised as a bent, old washerwoman, cursed and complained as she

followed her husband and daughter along just out of sight. If it hadn't been for the trained Guide Pigeon she'd sent after them, she would never have managed to find the way.

'Daddy, there's a pigeon following us,' said Betty. 'But then you already know that, don't you?'

'Pigeon, what pigeon?' Nerlin said, trying to look innocent and completely failing to do so.

There was a flapping of wings, and feathers drifted down from the sky as a fairly big eagle landed in front of them with a pigeon in its mouth.

'This one,' said Betty.

'Morning,' said the eagle.

'Good morning, eagle,' said Betty. 'You are not so much a carrier pigeon, as a pigeon carrier.'

'Do you want me to rip it to shreds, young mistress?' said the eagle.

'No, I don't think so,' said Betty. 'Why don't you fly as fast as you can right to the far end of Transylvania Waters, and pop the pigeon down on top of a nice high mountain?'

Mordonna had crept up through the

undergrowth just in time to see her Guide Pigeon carried off into the distance.

Oh yes, Miss Smartypants, think you've won, haven't you? Mordonna said to herself, and pulled a spare Guide Pigeon out of her washerwoman's rags.

This too was carried away by the eagle as soon as it returned, and so was the third. The final bird had been a mistake because it wasn't so much a Guide Pigeon as a Homing Pigeon, and once it was released from Mordonna's laundry bag, it simply turned round and flew straight back home.

Mordonna had only brought three spare pigeons, but she did have another trick up her sleeve. In fact, she had two – one up each sleeve. She had a pair of Guide Rats, and so she managed to keep on the trail of her daughter and husband right up until they reached Gertrude's hidden cave. By then, one of the Guide Rats had been skilfully and fairly painlessly converted into the eagle's lunch. The other rat was still working because the eagle had fallen fast asleep after its lunch due to the fact Mordonna had sprayed the second rat's fur with sleeping potion.

One up to me, I think, Mordonna said to herself, settling down to wait outside Gertrude's hideout.

'Your mother is hiding behind a tree, just across the clearing,' said Gertrude as Betty and Nerlin walked into the cave.

'Oh no!' said Betty.

'It's all right,' said Gertrude. 'I've given her something to keep her occupied.'

Then Gertrude and Nerlin hugged and cried a little, and Nerlin stopped feeling guilty about the killing-his-sister idea because he had completely dismissed it.

'My wife will try to kill you. We should do something,' said Nerlin, realising that blood was thicker than water and even if his brain was thicker than Mordonna's, there was no way he would help his wife destroy his sister, who he now realised he had missed more than he could imagine.

'It's all right, Nermie,' said Gertrude, using the childhood nickname she had given him. 'It's under control.'

'Oh, Germie, I have missed you,' said Nerlin.

Outside the cave was a loud noise that sounded as if every single swear word in the history of the world that had been collected together and stuffed inside Mordonna had been released. They poured out with such ferocity that all the leaves on the trees blushed bright red and fell off. As she cursed

and cursed and cursed, Mordonna tore off her filthy old washerwoman's disguise until she stood nearly naked outside the cave's entrance.

'Let's go and see what all that shouting's about, shall we?' said Gertrude.

As Gertrude, Nerlin and Betty emerged, there, standing in front of them, where someone who had once been the most beautiful and captivating witch in galaxies everywhere should have been, was a disgusting filthy old washerwoman.

But this was no disguise – this was Mordonna.

Everyone was speechless. Everyone except Betty, who tried so hard to stop laughing that she almost wet herself.

'You should cover yourself up, Mother,' she said, when she was finally able to speak. 'You could scare little children to death looking like that.'

Mordonna threw herself on the ground, screaming and cursing and banging her fists into the earth.

The eagle, who had slept off his potion, landed beside Mordonna, glanced at her once then twice

and said, 'I'm not carrying that off anywhere,' then fainted.

Somehow or other they managed to herd Mordonna into a small cave with a very strong door, where it was agreed they would leave her inside until she calmed down.

'Which,' as everyone said, 'could take years.'

'Of course,' said Betty, 'if we didn't feed her, she would calm down permanently, and it wouldn't take that long either.'

Fortunately that was a joke.

Later that night, when Nerlin had been tucked into bed, Gertrude took Betty down into the deepest cave and transferred the Ultimate Super-Wizard powers to her niece.

'I know I don't have to tell you not to abuse these awesome powers,' said Gertrude, 'but you can have a little fun with them if you want.'

She also transferred the Undo Button to Betty, but not to her forehead.[82]

---

[82] *No, it wasn't to anywhere rude. It's just that for security reasons I am not allowed to tell you where it was.*

THIS ILLUSTRATION HAS BEEN BLOCKED

By the PNS-ISA*

*Pathetic Neurotic Self-Important Security Agency

18

Although Betty said she'd do her auntie's makeover straight away, Gertrude decided to wait until everyone, especially Mordonna, had calmed down and all the who-was-going-to-be-King-or-Queen stuff had been sorted out.

'That's easy,' said Gertrude at breakfast the next day. 'I haven't the slightest desire to be Queen. You couldn't pay me to take the job.'

'I wouldn't mind even if you did want it,' said Nerlin. 'I just want to go up to the Enchanted Valley and take life easy. You know, keep a few chickens – ordinary ones, not magic ones – grow some flowers and sit in a big comfy chair looking down the mountain at the perfection that is Transylvania Waters.'

'Well, that's exactly what I want too,' said Gertrude. 'I don't suppose your cottage has a spare bedroom?'

Nerlin went a sort of mauve colour, which is like a human going white, but doesn't work for wizards who are white to start with. The thought of his sister moving into his peaceful cottage where he planned to spend the rest of his days was terrible.

Of course, Gertrude was just winding her brother up. Winchflat had already created the copy of the Enchanted Valley with a cottage for Gertrude, but neither Nerlin nor Mordonna knew that.

'Except,' Gertrude continued, 'I've only seen a little part of this land of wizards. I'd quite like to travel around for a bit before retiring in your Enchanted Valley. Though, I might find somewhere better during my travels.'

Getting the Ultimate Super-Wizard powers also meant getting a massive amount of incredible wisdom. While Betty decided she would take things slowly as she grew into her awesomeness, she did one tiny spell that removed any possible threat

of misunderstanding. She swapped Nerlin's and Gertrude's birthdays around. Nerlin became a bit older – which was what he felt, anyway – though Betty did fix his bad back while she was at it. And Gertrude became a bit younger, which was what she needed because she felt that after so many years in the drains, she had a lot of catching up to do.

It took Mordonna quite a while to calm down. Everyone thought they ought to feel a lot guiltier than they did about leaving her locked in the cave as a disgusting old washerwoman. It even took Nerlin, her loving husband, a few days before he began to feel sorry for her.

Finally, on Thursday afternoon, Nerlin went to the cave on his own and unlocked the door. He explained to Mordonna that Gertrude had no intention of claiming the throne and that she had transferred the Ultimate Super-Wizard powers to Betty – which made Mordonna want to explode – and that the first thing Betty had done with them had been to make Nerlin the oldest twin, which made Mordonna calm down and start coming to

terms with Betty being Queen.

'After all,' Mordonna said, 'it's quite a status symbol to be the Queen Mother.'

'It is indeed, my darling,' Nerlin agreed. 'Especially when you are the mother of not only the Queen of all witches and wizards, but of the witch who carries the Ultimate Super-Wizard powers – the only one who can undo the Washerwoman Spell and make you beautiful again.'

This did not take a lot of thinking about. When Mordonna had been turned into a wrinkled old hag, she knew that the Ultimate Super-Wizard powers were definitely real. What she didn't know was that Betty had done a few more special little spells that made the idea of Nerlin not being King and herself not being Queen anymore seem like quite a nice peaceful idea and the obvious thing to do. After all, which of Mordonna's children was the most like her?

Queen Betty.

There would be a great coronation. None of the Floods really wanted it, but it was sort of expected and everyone would've been so disappointed if they hadn't had one.

'And think of all the brilliant presents you'll get,' said Merlinmary.

'Oh, all right,' said Betty. 'But first, Auntie Gertrude and I are going to spend a few months taking a nice relaxing trip around Transylvania Waters. We'll do the coronation stuff when we get back.'

'Before you go, could you do me a favour?' asked Satanella.

'Of course,' said Betty, and changed her back into a small, black hairy dog.

Having realised how badly she had treated him, Satanella went searching for Tristram Jolyon De-Vere Creak to beg his forgiveness. She couldn't find him, and anyway, it was too late by then. Tristram had fallen in love with and married a small Belgian poodle called Lotte Marie Hanne Estlewurter.

Fortunately, the rule about only being able to

be any particular species[83] could be overturned by the holder of the Ultimate Super-Wizard powers,[84] and Betty had only been too happy to change Tristram back into a dog and together he and Lotte had gone to the most sophisticated resort in the Belgian seaside town of Knokke-Heist, where they lived happily ever after, having lots of weird-looking puppies and running a charming teashop for dogs where every customer got a free red rubber ball with their afternoon tea.

[83] *As it turns out, the 'Single Species' rule did not apply to Satanella. She had been a human when she'd been born, but it was only for two seconds.*

[84] *NONE of the rules about anything at all applied to the holder of the Ultimate Super-Wizard powers. There was only one single, simple rule for them: You Can Do Absolutely Anything You Want.*

19

The next morning, Queen Betty and Aunt Gertrude set off on their trip around Transylvania Waters. They didn't travel in great style with servants and carriages, but on two horses.

For six months they went from village to village, and then for six months after that they went from different villages to some more villages.

'I'm thinking,' Gertrude had said after the first six months, 'that maybe I'd like my makeover now. I might keep my eyes open for a boyfriend while we travel. I've never had one of them, so maybe I'll get more than one.'

And she did.

'And maybe,' Gertrude said to Betty, as they

went to Patagonia and travelled around there for a bit, 'you will find a husband.'

And did she?

VERY SPECIAL BISCUITS
HIGH-PROTEIN THERMO-NUCLEAR THUNDERPANTS RECIPE
INGREDIENTS
3 buckets of fresh [redacted]
1 cup of warm throbbing [redacted]
2 litres of three-week-old [redacted]
[redacted] to taste

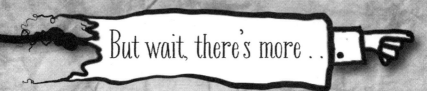

WINCHFLAT FLOOD'S WONDERFUL WORLD OF HATS

THE AMAZING HAT of INVISIBILITY

As you can see from this picture, the Hat of Invisibility is still a work in progress. Only the top of the wearer's head and other random holes around the body actually become invisible. This can be very embarrassing and messy, especially if you forget to take the hat off before you go to the toilet.

BETTY FLOOD'S TREASURY of BL***Y BRILLIANT SWEAR WORDS

Betty's absolutely top-favourite swear word is FL**BANNED**SM, which you have to admit is a pretty rude word. Her second best swear word is SCR**BANNED**WOB**BANNED**R, which is actually illegal to use in twenty-seven countries, though interestingly it is considered a term of endearment in Belgium.

TOP-SECRET TIP: Betty has hidden dozens of other swear words in the pages of this very book. They are broken up and cunningly disguised as parts of ordinary words. If you find them, you can join them up again and use them yourself.

Have you seen these other **INCREDIBLE** **FLOODS** books?

If not, why not? Write your pathetic excuse on the back of a $50 note and send it to Save the Children IMMEDIATELY, or you will turn into a shrivelled-up brussel-sprout.

THE FLOODS NEIGHBOURS

Colin Thompson

WINCHFLAT FLOOD'S WONDERFUL WORLD of HATS

THIS WEEK'S SPECIAL:
The Traffic Light Hat

Stop traffic whenever you feel like it, simply by standing in the road and using the remote control. Buses rushing by or ice-cream vans refusing to stop will be a thing of the past.

Order before Easter to get a traffic diverter bow tie absolutely free.

Only $99.99!!

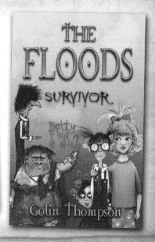

ULTIMATE SUPER-WIZARD POWERS

Ultimate Super-Wizard powers are the most powerful powers in the universe, from Belgium to the distant stars of Ursa Major and beyond.

You will probably never come across them because they only belong to one wizard at a time. Here is a typical example:

Normal, yet slightly clever human power as used by human ventriloquists – *throwing their own voice so it appears to come from across the room.*
Ordinary Wizard power – *throwing YOUR voice, so as you speak it appears to come from outside the room.*
Ultimate Super Wizard power – *throwing their own farts across the room so people think you did them.*

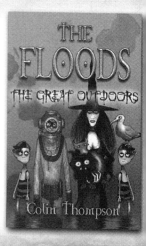

Things that **H**umans can do. Things that **W**izards can do and things that the wizard with the **U**ltimate **S**uper-**W**izard Powers can do.

EVENT	H	W	USW
Eat a fried egg underwater – with bacon (without being eaten by sharks) – without bacon		✓	✓
Make Vegemite taste nice			
UN-pop bubble wrap		✓	✓
UN-pop bubble wrap and fill each bubble with milk chocolate			✓
Learn by your mistakes		✓	✓
Think (insert your country here)'s Got Talent is really full of intelligent/useful/true people	✓		
Think everything will be all right	✓		*
Spell proply		✓	✓
Believe that one day there will/might be another FLOODS novel or two, perhaps	✓	✓	✓
Believe that even if there is NOT another FLOODS novel, there will be a BRILLIANT NEW sci-fi series **	✓	✓	✓

* Yes it will, as long as we get rid of all the Humans and Vegemite and Cardigans.

** Turn to the very last page.

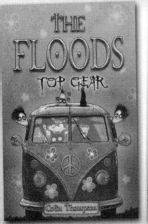

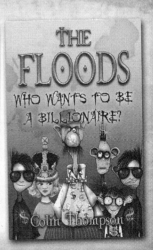

SOME UNUSUAL TRANSYLVANIA WATERS COMMUNITIES

THE LAVATORY GIANTS

This shy tribe of mountain dwellers are very seldom seen. Some people even say they are extinct or simply never existed. Not only are they over two metres tall, they also have enormous feet, which makes it impossible for them to ever find a nice pair of shoes. Because of this, they have taken to wearing lavatory pans on their feet and socks made out of carpets.

BIG TOE

INTERESTING TRUE FACT

About 30 years ago, I had a ceramics company and made quite a lot of money decorating washbasins, bidets and lavatory pans with real 24-carat GOLD!

and

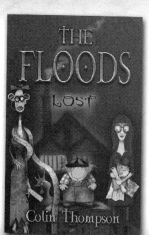

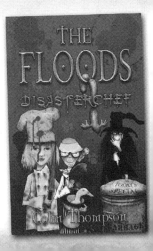

THE VALLEY OF LOST WIZARDS

It's hard to imagine anyone as clever as a witch or wizard would ever get lost, but it happens all the time. They wander off into the mountains to collect bits of slime, fungus and unwanted skin to use in their magic potions and, before they know it, the battery in their GPS has gone flat and they are completely lost. Yes, there are homing broomsticks, but most wizards are too technically stupid to use them. They wander about asking birds and frogs if they can help, but considering what wizards often do to birds and frogs, the creatures pretend they don't understand them. And because Transylvania Waters is a land of magic, every single lost witch and wizard eventually ends up in the Valley of Lost Wizards, and once they are in they can never get out. Their friends and families know from past cases that there is no point in sending out search parties because the valley itself is lost, not just in space, but in time too.

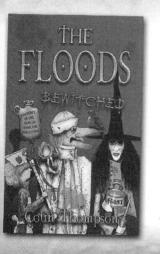

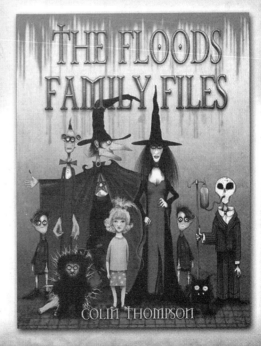

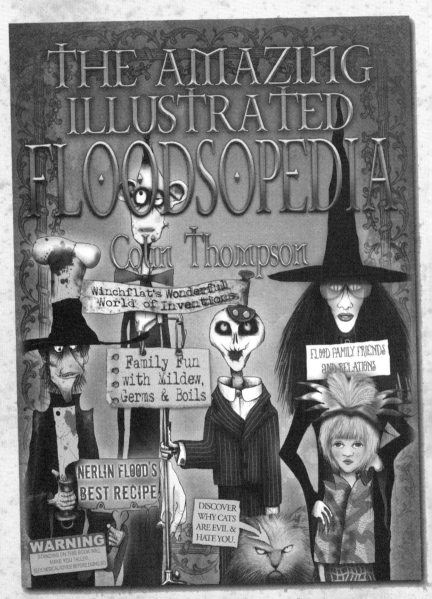

You need to get it immediately because it is impossible for you to ever realise just what a MASSIVE honour it is for you to have this book. Although Queen Scratchrot warned that it would end in tears, because they are the kindest, greatest wizards who have EVER lived, the Floods have decided to share their immense wisdomness, magic bacon-orientated secrets and history with you, even though you are mere, pathetic humans. Of course, they realise that even though you are mere, pathetic humans, lots of this book will be much too full of cleverness for you to understand, and by no means should you use this book without supervision and extremely strong pants.

JUST BY BEING IN THE SAME ROOM AS THIS BOOK, YOU WILL BE INSTANTLY CURED OF ALL DOOLALLYNESS AND FILLED WITH CLEVERNESS, BIO-DYNAMIC OZONE AND BACON.

JUST ASK YOURSELF — HOW MANY OTHER BOOKS COULD MAKE A PROMISE LIKE THAT?

AMAZING EXCLUSIVE OFFER ONLY AVAILABLE TO PEOPLE WITH A MONEY!! Buy THE AMAZING ILLUSTRATED FLOODSOPEDIA before the end of the months and get ALL the free air you can breathe for the rest of your life!!

'So what is coming after THE FLOODS?' I hear you ask.[*] Well, you need to . .

[*] I can't actually hear you asking this, thank goodness. If I could, it would mean you were in my house and that would be horrible and probably frighten my three ducks – Derek & the Dominos.